Mr. PuffBaLL

STUNT CAT TO THE STARS

Katherine Tegen Books is an imprint of HarperCollins Publishers.

Mr. Puffball: Stunt Cat to the Stars
Copyright © 2015 by Constance Lombardo
Library of Congress Cataloging-in-Publication Data
Lombardo, Constance.
  Stunt cat to the stars / Constance Lombardo. — First edition.
    Pages cm. — (Mr. Puffball ; #1)
  Summary: Mr. Puffball, a ten-month-old kitten who wants to be a movie star, leaves
home and makes his way to Hollywood, where he lands a job at Purramount Studios
working with his hero, El Gato, who turns out to be very different from what Mr.
Puffball expected.
  ISBN 978-0-06-232065-0 (hardcover)
  [1. Cats—Fiction. 2. Actors and actresses—Fiction. 3. Motion pictures—Production
and direction—Fiction. 4. Stunt performers—Fiction. 5. Self-confidence—Fiction.
6. Conduct of life—Fiction.] I. Title.
PZ7.1.L66Stu 2015   2014036065
[Fic]—dc23   CIP
                                                                             AC

Typography by Carla Weise
15 16 17 18 19   CG / RRDH   10 9 8 7 6 5 4 3 2 1
❖
First Edition

To Hank
and Madeline,
my two
favorite stars

My Early Years

My name is Mr. Puffball, and this is my story.

It all started in a little town called New Jersey, home to such famous American landmarks as my house. Back then, I was a mere kitten. But even an adorable kitten knows when he's different. While my siblings bounced in baskets and smelled things, I pretended— I was a brave knight, a mad scientist, a sad clown. I experimented with accents. I hummed showtunes.

Why? I didn't know.

Then one day, I saw an old movie on TV. It starred the world's greatest actor—*El Gato*. The movie opens on a dusty landscape filled with nothing but cactus, tumbleweeds, and UFOs. Into the frame saunters a pair of awesome cowboy boots. Slowly the camera pans up and up, until the screen is filled with the face of a tough-looking tabby. He swaggers toward a saloon, pushes past the swinging doors, holds up one bandaged arm, and says:

Wow!

That movie, *Cow-Cats & Aliens*, changed my life. Because suddenly I understood my destiny—to be a **MOVIE STAR ACTOR.** The very famous kind.

So I made a list of all I must do to become a movie star, and I called it:

ALL I MUST DO TO BECOME A MOVIE STAR

1. Act Like a Star. I made movie sets and arranged the lighting. Then I tricked my siblings into being my costars.

2. Dress Like a Star. I made costumes out of household items. A little glitter and glue could change a king into a ninja. An alien into a mailman. A wizard into a lizard.

3. Work on Acceptance Speech for Best Actor in an Excellent Movie. I rehearsed my speech for that night of all award nights: the Oscars.

4. Ignore the Naysayers. Sometimes my siblings refused to be in my shows. "This is dumb," they would say. "I'd rather chew stuff." Or, "Pile on Mr. Puffball!"

4

I tried ignoring them, which is hard when you're at the bottom of a kitten pileup. Or getting your ears gnawed. Or tweaked.

5. Envision a Movie Star Future. I spent hours on our couch, imagining my life—in show business!

My life was not easy. But the road to stardom never is.

A Star in the Family? Make That Two!

One day, I told Mom my plan. "I want to be a famous actor!" She nodded and said,

Then she whipped out an old photo.

CLEOCATRA MEETS
THE MUMMY!

It was Great-Grandma Zelda in a major motion picture. She looked so glamorous! And her acting, even in a photo, was superb. Hope stirred in my chest area. My own fur and blood had been a movie star. Perhaps I really would follow in her paw prints.

As if reading my mind, Mom smiled at me and said the words that would get stuck inside my head for the rest of my life. In a good way.

"Mr. Puffball, I believe you will be a star one day. If you follow your dreams."

And then, Mom gave me the best present ever: a replica of my hero, El Gato. He looked exactly like he did in *Cow-Cats & Aliens*. Only much smaller.

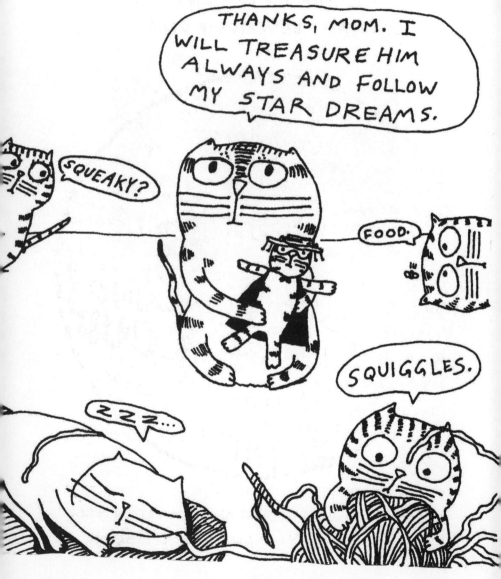

With Mom's encouragement, I decided it was time to get serious. So I made a pie chart of

THE SIX REASONS
I WILL BE A MOVIE STAR

Looking at my pie chart made me realize some-thing: I wanted a piece of pie. Preferably cherry.

From that day forward, my passion grew ever stronger. Tiny El Gato was my new costar as we acted out scenes from all my favorite movies.

Yes, tiny El Gato stuck by me during the good times and the bad. He never fell asleep during my monologues. He never stole my Tabby Treats. And he never complained if, in my excitement, a bit of my spit flew onto his cape. Because he understood that the show must go on, spit or no spit.

But even the best of times must end. Acting out scenes with tiny El Gato, home-made costumes, and zero sound equipment was not making me famous. No

NOW YOU SAY, "LUKE, I AM YOUR FATHER."

STARSHIP BY SCUITS

Hollywood talent scouts were coming over to say:

No camera-cats were filming my every move. No Hollywood directors were at my front door, saying:

So one day, after I'd checked the front door for directors, I decided that if Hollywood wouldn't come to me, I'd go to Hollywood. But it's not easy to leave the comforts of home. I needed that extra push. And a push is what I got.

It happened when my sister pushed me. I skidded across the room into a pile of newspapers, knocking the top one loose. As the newspaper floated down, my mood changed from grumpy to happy:

My moment of truth had arrived. I glanced at the newspaper. Then I glanced at my siblings, who were rolling around making poopy noises. Then I asked myself, "What would Furlock Holmes do? What would Hairy Pawter do? What would Catman do?"

They'd go to that audition! And they wouldn't tell their moms, just like I wouldn't tell mine. Because she'd say, "But you're just an adorable little kitten. You can't go to Hollywood. At least let me knit you a sweater first." And that would take forever!

Besides, I wasn't a kitten anymore. I was fourteen months old. Plus, I was mature for my age. So I found a strip of cloth and tied it around my waist. I tucked tiny El Gato inside, along with my newspaper clipping, my photo of Great-Grandma Zelda, and some yogurt-covered mouse tails.

Mom was watching a yoga video and didn't see me mouth the words *Good-bye, Mom.* Nor did she see me scribble this note:

Then I padded out the back door.

When I reached the corner, I turned and looked at my old home. A big part of me wanted to race back, get a forehead lick from Mom, and play Chew the Tail with my siblings.

But a bigger part of me knew it was time to go.

An even bigger part of me, all of me in fact, was chased farther from home by a large dog. Fortunately, she chased me in a westerly direction. So, even after that dog got bored chasing me, I just kept going.

My Journey in Postcards
(to Mom)

As I made my way across this great land of ours, I sent postcards back to Mom.

from the heart of
PENNSYLVANIA

DEAR MOM, APRIL
WALKING FROM NJ
TO PA IS HARD. BUT THEN
THESE NICE CATS LET
ME USE THEIR BUGGY.
WOW! MY NEW PA
FRIENDS ALWAYS WEAR
BLACK. I THINK
THEY'RE GOTH!
MISS YOU! LOVE, YOUR
TRAVELING SON,
Mr. Puffball

SHARK 39

TO:
MOM of Mr. PuffBALL
LiTTLE YELLOW HOUSE
NEW JERSEY
USA

WEST VIRGINIA IS FOR BLU...

DEAR MOM,
This LARGE FELLOW IS THE **STATE ANIMAL**. HE WAS HAPPY TO GIVE ME A RIDE — UNTIL HE FOUND ME. WHEN he DID, he CLEARLY THOUGHT I was "UNBEARABLE." (GET IT?) LOVE, YOUR PUNNY SON, Mr. Puffball

HAIRY PAWTER — COOL!

MOM of Mr. PuffBall
LiTTLE YELLOW HOUSE
NEW JERSEY
USA

P.S. MAYBE I'll be on a STAMP ONE DAY! ☆

END OF APRIL

DEAR MOM,
THE KENTUCKY DERBY IS NOT A **HAT!** AFTER THE **RACE** (NOT HAT) MY PAL **SPEEDO** TOOK ME TO THE STATE LINE IN EXCHANGE FOR SOME **SUGAR CUBES**. THAT'S WHAT I CALL A **SWEET DEAL!** LOVE, YOUR GALLOPING SON, Mr. Puffball
XXX O

WOW!!
EL GATO 39

POST CARD

MOM of M...
LiTTLE YE...
NEW

Greetings from KENTUCKY

DATE UNSURE
DEAREST MOM,
    MISSOURI IS WHERE THE
WRITER OF **LITTLE MOUSE** ON THE
PRAIRIE WAS BORN. IT'S A COOKBOOK.
MISSOURI IS ALSO KNOWN AS "**THE
SHOW ME STATE**". I JUST WISH
SOMEBODY WOULD "**SHOW ME**" HOW
TO LAND THIS THING. OH MY!

HERE COMES A
TORNADO.
WHOOSH!
HOLD ON TIGHT!

LOVE, YOUR
HIGH-FLYING
SON,
Mr. Puffball

Mom of me (MR. P)
LITTLE YELLOW HOUSE
IN NEW JERSEY
                USA

GROUCHY 39
CAT

GREETINGS FROM
KANSAS

DEAR MOM,   MAY-15H
    NOW I KNOW I'M NOT IN
NEW JERSEY ANYMORE - I JUST
TORNADOED ACROSS **KANSAS!**
THEIR STATE MOTTO IS "**AD
ASTRA PER ASPERA**." IT MEANS
"TO THE STARS THROUGH HARD-
SHIP." PERFECT, RIGHT?
YOUR DIZZY SON, Mr. Puffball

IS THERE
AN OLD
JERSEY?

MOM o' PUFFBALL
LITTLE YELLOW HOUSE
NEW JERSEY
           USA

17

BRRR! FROM COLO-RADO

DEAR MOM,
    HERE I AM ATOP A HUGE SKI SLOPE. HOW WILL I GET DOWN? Here COMES SOMEONE. A SKI INSTRUCTOR, PERHAPS?
ME: "CAN YOU HELP ME?"
HIM: "SURE!" (PUSH)
ME: "AAAAAAA AAAAAAAAAA AAAAHHHHH!"
(WIPEOUT)
LOVE, YOUR SNOW-COVERED SON,
Mr. Puffball

MAYBE MAY

MOM of Mr. P-BALL
Little Yellow House
NEW JERSEY
P.S. BRRR. USA
♡ ♡ ♡ ♡ ♡ ♡ ♡ ♡
HAPPY MOM'S DAY! ♡

←UFO GREETINGS, EARTHLING. FROM ROSWELL, NEW MEXICO!

I ♥ NEW MEXICO

I ♥ OUTER SPACE

A WRINLE IN TIME (JUNE)

DEAR MOM,
THIS ALIEN GUY CRASHED HIS SPACESHIP INTO THE DESERT IN 1947 AND HASN'T LEFT SINCE! NOW HE USES HIS "UFO" TO GIVE RIDES ACROSS THE UNI-VERSE AND BACK. THAT'S TOP SECRET, BTW.
LOVE, YOUR INTERGALACTIC SON, Mr. Puffball ← FUN!

ALIEN LIFE FORM?←

TO:
MOM of MR. P-B
LITTLE YELLOW HOUSE
NEW JERSEY
EASTERN SEABOARD
UNITED STATES of AMERICA
PLANET EARTH
THE MILKY WAY
GALAXY

I CROSSED THE GRAND CANYON, ARIZONA!

SUMMER

DEAR MOM,
When this BIRD GRABBED ME, I THOUGHT He WAS THAT ARIZONA PHOENIX YOU HEAR ABOUT. ACTUALLY, HE WANTED ME FOR DINNER. I STOPPED HIM WITH AN **AWESOME** EL GATO IMPRESSION. GOOD THING CONDORS LIKE WESTERNS! MISS YOU AND **LOVE**, YOUR QUICK-THINKING SON, Mr. Puffballs

NON-SCARY BIRD →

39

TO: MY MOM
LITTLE YELLOW HOUSE
NEW JERSEY
USA
P.S. THANKS, POSTAL CAT!

The condor surprised me with a gift from a former "dinner guest." It was a skateboard. I'd never skated before, but when the condor told me he was getting hungry, you should have seen me jump on it and go!

Skateboarding is the best! I kicked, twisted, and grinded my way across Arizona with the wind rushing through my fur. And soon, tiny El Gato and I ollied over the state line into California. Oh, how we cheered!

We were almost in Hollywood.

An Unexpected Detour

The next day, after some rad skateboarding, I saw the sign I'd dreamed of since kittenhood. Some locals were waiting to greet me and maybe give me a free map of celebrity homes. Or at least a high five. I couldn't believe tiny El Gato and I were finally in Hollywood.

Or were we?

My first moments in Hobowood were tense. I feared I'd said the wrong thing.

But then—

They liked me! And I liked them. The hobos were free spirits who lived by their own rules, eating beans right out of the can and wandering the nearby forest, which they called Nature's Litterbox.

We sat down together to stuff our faces with beans. When we were done eating, they said, "And now, it's showtime!" I anticipated more gas-related frivolity, but I was wrong. My new friends put on a genuine hobo show.

Of course I had to join in. A large stick became a wand for my rendition of Hairy Pawter. I covered my paws with empty bean cans for RoboCat and used my skateboard for a reenactment of *The Secret Life of Walter Kitty.*

I was having so much fun that I didn't notice the hobos stop performing to stare at me. But I sure noticed when they clapped and yelled, "Bravo!" Wow. I'd traveled across the country in search of stardom, and here in Hobowood, I'd become an overnight sensation. And the sun hadn't even set yet.

"Teach us, Mr. Puffball!" said the hobos. "Teach us everything you know!"

Let's face it. After all the movies I'd watched, I did know a lot. I could stay in Hobowood and become an acting teacher by day, an American Hobo Idol by night. I would write scripts on tree bark, make a director's chair out of sticks, and create costumes out of leaves. Maybe I'd even carve an Oscar out of stone.

As if on cue, the head hobo put his arm around me and said, "Mr. Puffball, you have the heart of a hobo. Please stay with us forever."

Silently, the hobos linked paws to form a circle around me and began to sing the hobo initiation song:

Life with the hobos is living
    pure and free,
We travel round by train
    and sleep under tree,
Oh, never do we want for
    anything you see,
Because we're the best that
    great cats be!

Suddenly the world stood still as the last line of their song ran over and over in my mind—"Because we're the best that great cats be! . . . that great cats be . . . great cats be . . ."

"*The Great Catsby!*" I yelled. "I have to get to my audition!"

"An audition to become a hobo?" said one of the hobos.

"No," I said firmly, "an audition to become a Hollywood movie star. In Hollywood."

She broke from the circle and put her arm around me. They did that a lot. "We love you, Mr. Puffball," she said. "And if you really want to go to Hollywood, we're gonna help you get there."

So the next morning, my new hobo friends and I said our tearful good-byes. I gave them my skateboard, which was very nice of me. And they put me . . .

on a train,

hobo-style.

Which was very nice of them.

As the train chugged along the California coast, I realized Destiny was close at hand. (And I don't mean the cat sleeping nearby whose name happened to be Destiny.) My joy rang out in a yowl heard round the world. Or at least inside the train car.

Hours later, Destiny and my other new friends said, "One, two, three, heave!" and off I flew. To the Real Sign. The Right Sign.

I bounced off the *W* and landed like cats always land: on my feet. And there I was, on that dusty California hillside that had been the site of such famous movies as:

ROAR!

GODZILLA
VERSUS
HOLLYWOOD

AND:

KING KONG
VISITS
AMERICAN LANDMARKS

HOLLYWOOD

Lost in these celluloid dreams, I was caught off guard by a strong breeze coming up from the valley that almost blew me and my little buddy away.

A newspaper landed on my face. And inside was a very important message that seemed written just for me—

So I walked down the hill and on and on until I was in the heart of downtown Hollywood. Then I asked for directions.

And there it was—the most glamorous groomery in the world. I would walk through those doors a nobody. But I would come out looking—and probably smelling—like a star.

5
Becoming Divine

Inside, an ultra-fancy cat with an unusual accent said, "So, you want for Ms. Lola to make you divine?"

"Yes, please," I said.

Ms. Lola looked me over like I was a cupcake she was about to decorate. Then she summoned her support staff.

We began with a thorough cleansing.

Then Ms. Lola whipped out her megapower fur-dryer, set it to "hurricane," and let 'er rip.

Soon she was elbow deep in my fur, fluffing me like I'd never been fluffed before. Next came a major smooth-down with Aqua-Fur Deluxe Gel for Males.

Then my true makeover began.

"You want movie star style?" asked Ms. Lola, glancing at tiny El Gato.

"Absolutely," I said.

"Good," said Ms. Lola. "You are in the paws of a cat who shaped many movie star heads and body furs." She proceeded to experiment on me with styles I didn't even know were possible for a tabby.

Yes, I was braided, beaded, dyed, spectacled, and dressed in black, but nothing felt right. Then she tried a style that would have been perfect for those old silent films where someone tied to train tracks yells, "Help! Help! Won't somebody with a huge moustache please rescue me?"

5. DASHING.

I was losing hope. It seemed Ms. Lola had run out of ideas. But then she snipped her ruby scissors together three times and said:

I was leading-man handsome. Opening-night handsome. Run-away-from-paparazzi handsome. *Handsome Tabby* magazine handsome. And I was ready to take Hollywood by storm.

"Thank you, Ms. Lola," I said.

"Very welcome, Mr. Poofball. Now, go wow them. And if ever you write a Hollywood memoir, please to make one chapter about me."

I promised her I would. Then I asked for directions to Metro-Golden-Meower Studios (otherwise known as MGM).

"Really?" I asked.

"Not really," said Ms. Lola. "But here's something really to follow." And she handed me this map and instructions:

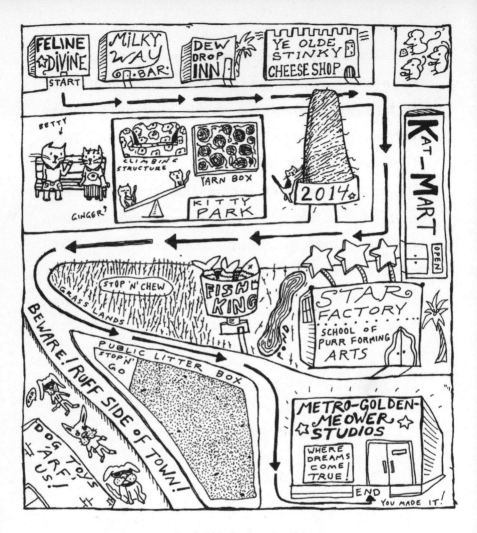

DIRECTIONS TO
METRO-GOLDEN-MEOWER STUDIOS
(also known as MGM)

Exit **Feline Divine.** (Come back soon!) Turn Left toward **Milky Way Bar.** Hold your nose as you pass the **Ye Olde Stinky Cheese Shop**. Don't eat **the mice** on the corner. (They're unemployed actors.) Ignore **Kat-Mart**. (Not fancy!) See the world's biggest **scratching post**? Resist the urge! (Unless you want fleas.) Wave at the cuties in **Kitty Park**. Say "Meow" to Hollywood fixtures **Betty and Ginger on their bench.** If they offer advice, take it! Mewly Cyrus sure did! Sharp Left! **Bad Dogs!** Hiss! Enjoy the grass at the **Stop 'n' Chew**. Then **Stop 'n' Go** at the public litter box. (There's a clean spot in there somewhere!) **Fish King** = delish! Hey—it's the **Star Factory** (where cats learn how to be fabulous). And now . . . ta-da!—**You Are There!** (If you're good at reading maps.)

I followed Ms. Lola's instructions step by step. When I reached the end, I glanced up and—

I, Mr. Puffball, was standing before Metro-Golden-Meower Studios. As the setting sun bathed me in its golden light, I thought about my life so far—from my daydreaming couch to my cross-country trek to Hobowood to Feline Divine to this: the place where my audition—and my future—awaited.

Suddenly, I heard the sound of drums. Then I realized it was the sound of my heart beating in my ears. There was only one thing to do: yoga. All the best actors do it. So I took a deep breath and got into tree pose.

OM.

Hours later, I uncurled my limbs and found a place to sleep, since the audition wasn't until morning. It was not the Beverly Hills Hotel, but it would do. *Tonight I dream*, I thought as I drifted off to sleep, *but tomorrow my dreams come true.*

CATS ALLEY
NO DOGS

SOON WE'LL SLEEP ON SILK SHEETS LIKE REAL STARS. RIGHT, EL GATO?

ZZZ

KRUMB KANDY INC.

WORLD CARDBOARD... WE'U GOT COVERED!

ZZZ

ACME SOAP CAKES

The Not-So-Great Catsby

The next morning, I carefully groomed myself for my debut audition.

And mentally reviewed the advice Betty and Ginger from the map had given me the day before:

FLASHBACK

STARRING BETTY + GINGER

GOING TO AN AUDITION? TAKE OUR ADVICE... MEWLY CYRUS SURE DID.

STAND STRAIGHT! HOLLYWOOD IS NOT LOOKING FOR SLOUCHERS!

SPEAK CLEARLY! HOLLYWOOD IS NOT LOOKING FOR MUMBLERS.

BE ASSERTIVE! HOLLYWOOD IS NOT LOOKING FOR WIMPY CATS.

BE YOURSELF! HOLLYWOOD IS NOT LOOKING FOR COPY CATS.

NICE BOW TIE! YOU SHOULD GET A SWEATER VEST.

AND LEARN TAP DANCING. WE LOVE TAP DANCING!

AND SOUP. COULD YOU BRING US SOME SOUP?

TOMATO IS OUR FAVORITE...

YOU SHOULD EAT MORE SOUP.

I stood up straight and strode assertively to the front door of MGM Studios, where I was startled to see the place looking a bit less excellent than I had originally thought.

No matter. Perhaps they were too busy making blockbuster movies to bother with building upkeep. I knocked on the door. A slat opened and two golden eyes appeared.

I cleared my throat and said, "I am Mr. Puffball, and I am here for the audition."

"What say?" croaked the voice behind the door.

"I am Mr. Puffball, and I am here for the audition," I said, louder this time.

The door creaked open. And there stood someone whom I can only describe as very extremely old.

He looked me over with his ancient, hairy face and said, "What the *Blazing Saddles* do you want?"

"I want to audition . . . ," I said.

"Speak up, sonny," he said. "Into the ear trumpet, please. My hearing is *Gone with the Wind*."

"I'm here to audition for *The Great Catsby*!"

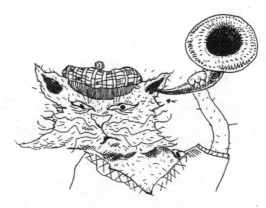

"Oh!" he said at last. *The Great Catsby.* Why didn't you say so? Sure, I remember that audition."

"You mean I missed it?"

"Yup," he said. "You missed it by—let me consult my timepiece—about twenty years."

And then he laughed, with his big yellow-toothed mouth wide open. While my whole world came crashing down.

"But the newspaper . . . with the casting call . . . look . . . ," I said, carefully unfolding it. As I handed the clipping to the elderly tomcat, I realized the newspaper may not have been a recent issue. In fact, it was so old and brittle, it cracked and broke into a million little pieces. Just like my dreams.

The old cat grabbed a piece, gobbled it down, and said, "I believe that Girl Scout cookie was stale."

"Yes," I said, slumping to the ground. "Very stale."

Something to Purr About

I laid my head on a rock, closed my eyes, and said farewell to my hopes and dreams.

The old tom tapped my head with his cane and said, "Why so glum, chum?"

"You wouldn't understand," I sighed.

"Try me," he said.

So I opened my eyes and told him my whole sob story. He switched on his hearing aid so I didn't have to shout.

"So you see," I said, "I came. I tried. I missed it. My life is now over. Good-bye."

"Hogwarts!" he said. "So you missed one audition. Somewhere in this crazy town there's a better one just waiting for a cat named Mr. Puffball."

"But where?" I asked.

"How about over there?" he said. "They got auditions by the bucketful."

47

He pointed across the street, and this is what I saw:

The neon lights of Purramount Studios flashed as bright as Glinda the Good Witch, making me feel like I was wearing magic slippers and could do anything. "There's no place like Hollywood!" I said, jumping up.

"Let's go! Because this crazy town needs me like the Tin Man needs a heart. Thanks, Mr., uh—"

"Chester P. Grumpus the Third. But you can call me Chet."

"Grumpus? Like the famous movie director who made such great films as *Catsablanca?*"

"That's me," he said. "Time sure has gone by."

"*The Sound of Meowsic?*"

"Those hills sure were alive."

"She was a huge star," said Chet. "But my favorite movie will always be my first: *Cleocatra Meets the Mummy.*"

"Cleocatra was my great-grandma Zelda!" I said.

"I thought you looked familiar," said Chet. "You've got her stripes. Now, let's get you to Purramount Studios and see if you've got any of her talent."

And that was how my friend Chester P. Grumpus III (but you can call him Chet) directed me to my first audition. Sadly, it was a private audition for the romantic comedy *Take Me to the Cat Spa*, and they wouldn't let us in. So Chet scooted us around back and tapped out a secret knock. The door opened, and there stood the janitor.

Chet introduced us and said, "Whiskers used to be a famous Hollywood dancer. He certainly used to sweep the ladies off their paws."

Whiskers snuck me into Purra-mount Studios in a very clever way.

And there I was at my first Hollywood audition! The director called us up, one by one, to act with all the drama of a true movie star.

The rest is history. I still remember the headlines:

Take Me to the Cat Spa was a hit. Everybody in it won an Oscar and made tons of money. For me, there was only one problem—I was not in *Take Me to the Cat Spa*. Because, at the audition, just as I began my monologue:

I heard a bone-chilling sound—

Then all the "experienced actors" started laughing, and I was trapped in my own worst nightmare.

Whiskers whisked me out of there before my tears caused significant water damage to the floor. Outside, Chet was waiting, hoping for good news.

"*A Star Is Born?*" he asked.

I was too miserable to answer. So Whiskers spoke up. "Actually, we had to *Bolt*. Poor little Puffball."

(Cue the sad violins.)

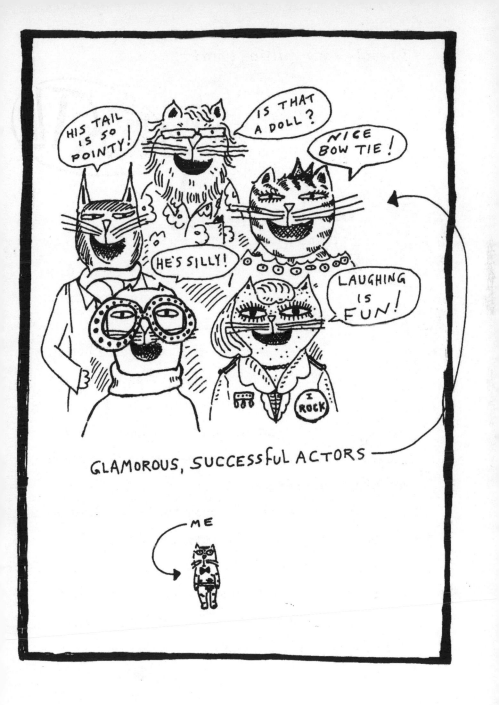

My Life, the Musical

Chet and Whiskers took me back to MGM Studios. Chet said, "I'll make us some chow." Whiskers said, "And I'll provide the entertainment." He went into another room and came back in a surprising outfit.

Soon Chet brought out the food. I like food. Plus the music had cheered me up. The day's disaster was becoming a distant memory.

Until Chet said, "So you messed up that audition good and plenty?"

"I wasn't *that* bad."

"No, not bad," said Whiskers. "Awful."

"Smelly as rotten bananas?" said Chet.

"Stinky as Rottweiler breath," said Whiskers.

56

"Pungent as Whiskers' dirty laundry?" said Chet.

Fortunately, I was saved from more odorous comparisons by the entrance of a she-cat.

"Hello, Kitty," said Chet.

"Kitty LaRue bunks here with us," said Whiskers. "She used to be a famous Hollywood chanteuse. Now the only notes she delivers are singing telegrams."

"Kitty, meet Mr. Puffball," said Chet. "Today was his first audition, and frankly, Kitty, he stunk."

"Like forgotten-in-the-back-of-the-fridge milk?"

We all nodded.

"He's got quite a face," said Kitty, looking me over. "And a bow tie to beat the band. Can you sing, kid?"

"I never tried," I said.

"Can you dance?" asked Whiskers.

"I don't know."

"Can you deliver a line so full of feeling it makes grown cats weep?" asked Chet.

"I thought I could," I said. "Now I'm not so sure."

"Mr. Puffball," said Kitty, "what you need is schooling."

"I saw the Star Factory across the street, but I don't have any money."

"We got school right here," said Whiskers.

"*Telegram for Mr. Puffball,*" sang Kitty.

Kitty sang like an angel.

Then Chet stepped up. He sang like a sick donkey.

Next Whiskers crooned:

I was so swept up in the magic of the musical number, I joined the Hollywood chorus:

Then it was time for my solo. I got down on one knee, threw my arms open wide, and belted out:

I stopped. Because I heard a sound that shook me to my very core. Like a big-toothed saw on solid granite.

So I stuffed cotton in my ears, curled up in a comfy basket, and sighed. It had been a long, difficult day, followed by a wonderful, musical evening. Now I would sleep in a cozy room, surrounded by friends, with new hope in my heart. As I drifted toward dreamland, I couldn't resist purring out a few more lines. Because every great musical scene needs a big finale:

And then, with the help of the earplugs, a heavenly silence filled the air.

Educating Mr. Puffball

The next day, Chet woke me with a poke or three of his cane and handed me a piece of paper.

"You know what you'll be after two weeks of this schedule?" asked Chet, once I finished reading it.

"Very tired?" I said.

"You'll be a triple threat—a cat who can act, sing, and dance."

"Excellent," I said. "Let's get started."

"Here's the first item of business," said Chet, handing me a bran muffin. "Now you're good to go."

SCHEDULE TO PERFECT MR. PUFFBALL

7:00—7:30 Breakfast.
> The early cat gets the worm! Of course, we don't eat worms around here. Most mornings it's oatmeal or a bran muffin.

7:30—9:30 Act Up!
Instructor: Chester P. Grumpus III (Chet)
Class description: You will vocalize, emote, gesture, express, etc., until you have mastered the Fine Art of Acting (or at least no longer stink).

10:00—12:00 Make a Joyful Noise!
Instructor: Kitty LaRue
Class description: You will practice your scales until you can sing E major in a minor key in no time flat.

12:00—1:00 Lunch.
> Our backyard pond and rudimentary fishing pole will help you stock our daily all-we-can-eat lunch buffet!

1:00—3:00 Shall We Dance?
Instructor: Whiskers
Class description: Shake your hips! Move your tail! Jazz hands! We'll dance like nobody's watching (but I will be watching you).

3:00—4:00 Nap. (Or yoga.)
4:15—5:00 Dinner Show!
(See Whiskers for your grass skirt and lei.)

Chet said school should be fun—like a board game!
And it was:

THE GAME OF SCHOOL ☆

OOPS! YOU **STOMP** ON WHISKERS' TAIL WHILE ATTEMPTING A COMPLICATED **TAP DANCE** ROUTINE. **SKIP A TURN.** (AND GET HIM A BANDAGE.)

☆ YOU SING ☆ "SOMEWHERE OVER THE RAINBOW" IN TUNE, BACKWARD, AND IN FRENCH. MOVE AHEAD ☆ ☆ TWO SPACES.

YOU ENUNCIATE "I'M NOT A BIG, FAT PANDA; I'M **THE** BIG, FAT PANDA!" FROM DEEP INSIDE A PANDA SUIT. ☆ MOVE AHEAD ONE SPACE. ☆ ☆

YOU SCREAM "IT'S ALIVE! IT'S ALIVE!" WITH THE FERVOR OF A **MAD SCIENTIST!** ☆ MOVE AHEAD ONE SPACE. ☆

YOU SUCCESSFULLY HOLD 8 MARBLES IN YOUR MOUTH WHILE SINGING "**THE RAIN IN SPAIN STAYS MAINLY IN THE PLAIN.**" ☆ MOVE AHEAD BUT SPIT OUT THE MARBLES FIRST.

START

$\frac{1}{2}$ WAY

You FORGET THE WORDS TO "CABARET" AND ACCIDENTALLY SING "LIFE IS A CAT BERET." 🐱 MOVE BACK THREE SPACES.

YOU RECITE THE ENTIRE THIRD ACT of **A TALE OF TWO KITTIES** WHILE IN BRIDGE POSE. ☆

OM! MOVE AHEAD 2 SPACES

YOU SWALLOW THE MARBLES! GO DIRECTLY TO THE LITTER BOX. DO NOT PASS GO. DO NOT COLLECT $100. **OUCH!**

THERE!

THE DISCO BALL YOU GOT AT A YARD SALE MAKES CHET DIZZY.

SELL IT ON C-BAY.

YOU DANCE, ACT, AND SING YOUR WAY THROUGH A **LIVELY** RENDITION OF "ROMEO AND JULIE-CAT." CROSS THE FINISH LINE!

☆ CONGRATULATIONS, GRADUATE! ☆

On graduation day, I staged a one-cat show of *The Lord of the Rings, the Musical*!

"Mr. Puffball, your singing wizard was magical!"

"Your portrayal of Gollum was precious!"

"That dancing-with-orcs number was brilliant!"

"You're ready for the movies!" they all said.

"There's an audition at Purramount tomorrow," said Whiskers, "and you don't have to get there by mop bucket. I've told the director all about you."

Happy tears filled my eyes. "You guys are the bestest friends a cat could have. I'm going to that audition tomorrow to make you proud."

Then they gathered around me in what actors refer to as a "group hug."

Sweet.

Audition: Take Two

My lines were memorized, my scales sung, my feet licked clean, and my bow tie perfect. Purramount Studios was about to meet Mr. Puffball and his Star Qualities.

I looked at my tiny El Gato and made a quick mental list of what an actor wears to an audition and called it:

WHAT AN ACTOR WEARS
TO AN AUDITION

1. A classic black bow tie
2. Neatly combed fur
3. A winning smile
4. ~~My tiny El Gato doll Mom gave me~~

I untied tiny El Gato and handed him to Chet. "Take good care of him," I said.

"Will do," said Chet.

As I looked back to mouth a silent good-bye to tiny El Gato, I saw Chet setting up the checkers set. *Hmmm.* Then Whiskers and I trotted over to Purramount Studios. He had to go to work. And so did I.

"Remember, it's tap, twirl, smile," said Whiskers. "Speak clearly. With feeling. Always look at your audience . . ."

". . . and twitch my tail for emphasis," I said.

"Now you're thinking like an actor, Mr. Puffball."

When I strode into the audition room, it was the same as before. *But I was not.* Now I had studied with some of the best cats in the business. So when Director DeMew called, "You're up, Mr. Puffball!" I confidently crooned a few verses from *My Fair Kitty,*

recited dramatically
from *Downton Tabby*,

and finished with
an impressive tap
routine.

Let's face it. I was awesome. So I was not surprised to be one of the few selected for the next round of auditioning. Director DeMew called us over one by one.

"So, Mr. Puffball," she asked when it was my turn, "why do you want to be in my movie, *Nine Lives to Live?*"

Easy. "Because I want to be a movie star."

Next, Director DeMew said, "Let's see a slow twirl." Lucky for me, I'd gone to Whiskers' extra-credit class, How to Do a Slow Twirl.

Several cats were told "Thanks, but no thanks." But not I. Then Director DeMew yowled, "Now some facial expressions!"

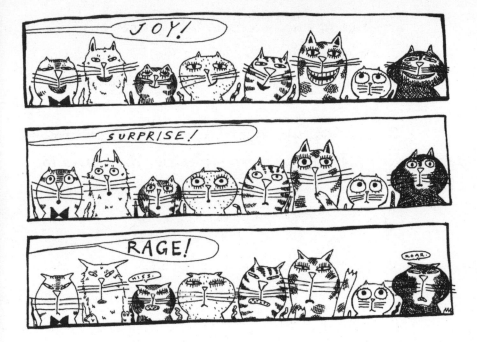

Only one more name would be called that day, and that cat would *not* be in *Nine Lives to Live*. My ears burned with anticipation as Director DeMew said, "Thanks, but no thanks, Mr. Puff . . . *ah, ah, ah, achoo!* . . . Mr. Puffbaby."

Mr. Puffbaby was out, and I was in! We all did a happy dance (except Mr. Puffbaby, who left looking bummed). We were going to be in the movie *Nine Lives to Live*! I was grinning like the Cheshire Cat as Director DeMew handed us our roles—

Purramount Studios ☆

PRODUCTION:
NiNE LiVES TO LiVE!

DIRECTOR: CECELIA B. DEMEW

OPEN AUDITION ASSIGNMENTS

NAME: MR. Puffball

PART: EXTRA

SCHEDULE: 8:00 - 8:00
DAILY

IMPORTANT

NO HISSING, YOWLING, MEWLING,
HAIRBALLS, CAT FIGHTS, OR
BITING ON THE SET.

I thanked the director and skipped home. Chet, Whiskers, and Kitty were all waiting for my news. I held up my happy paper and said, "I got the part!"

"Does that say 'Extra'?" asked Chet.

"It says Extra!" I said. "In the upcoming film *Nine Lives to Live*, I play a character named Extra."

"I don't think so," said Kitty.

"Maybe I get extra money," I said.

"Definitely not," said Whiskers.

"Extra," said Chet, "means you've been cast as an extra. One of the crowd."

"What's important," said Kitty, "is that you're going to be in a movie!"

"When will I get my lines?"

"No lines," said Chet. "Extras do not speak."

"Do they sing?"

"Nope," said Chet. "Mostly you mill about, not drawing attention to yourself."

"You might bust a move," said Whiskers.

"Really?" I asked.

"Probably not."

I was not going to speak or sing or dance in this movie. I was not going to be rich or famous. I was going to laugh when the real actors said something funny, gasp when the real actors did something surprising, and cry when one of the real actors stepped on my tail on his way to the lunch buffet.

It almost got me down. But then I remembered the great extras of cinematic history:

BACKGROUND
munchkin

RANDOM
HOBBIT

THAT WEIRD ALIEN
IN STAR WARS

"This is not my dream coming true," I said. "But I suppose it's better than a poke in the eye."

"You know what's also better than a poke in the eye?" said Kitty.

"Conga line!" said Whiskers.

Wherein I Climb Every Mountain (Or at Least One)

Prepare to be amazed. You're about to enter a world where things happen that, frankly, you didn't think would happen. Because that's what Hollywood is all about:

THE ELEMENT OF... SURPRISE!

Picture me on that first day as I stroll over to Purramount: sun shining, birds chirping, bran muffin digesting. Along the way, I practice my facial expressions—happiness, grouchiness, confusion, hunger. I'm ready for anything. Except the unexpected.

I arrive on the set of *Nine Lives to Live* and greet

the other extras. Director DeMew comes out, raises her megaphone, and says, "Extras! Follow directions! Act like a crowd! No bathing on camera! And, most of all, DO NOT BOTHER THE STAR!"

Now I'm curious. Who is the star? I didn't know yet and neither do you.

Next a door swings open and slams shut, followed by the distinctive sound of cowboy boots clicking across the floor. And then, do I imagine it? Or is that the *swoosh* of a long black cape? I prick up my ears and hear excited murmurs spring up from the extras all around me.

Someone gasps.

Another cat faints.

Or is simply sleeping.

Someone stage-whispers, "It's him!" And every green and gold eye in the house (except for the sleeping cat) is turned in one direction like eyes seeing something very, very interesting. I search for the object of their attention, but there are many extras in front of me, some with heads so big they block my view.

So I elbow my way through the crowd. The camera (if a camera had been following me at that moment) pans right as I elbow, elbow, and elbow. Someone says, "Ow." And I say, "Sorry." Someone says, "Watch it, fella." And I say, "Watch yourself, buddy." And so on, until I have left the sea of extras behind and the amazing thing is revealed in one astounding moment.

My eyes go wide. Because this is who I saw in the studio that fateful day, not more than ten paws away from me (cue orchestral music):

I gasped, of course. But El Gato did not even glance my way. So I coughed very loudly. *Still* he did not notice me. So I sneezed as violently as possible.

Then I sang "You Are My Sunshine" while dancing the cha-cha-cha.

Nothing.

To the great cat himself, I was just another extra. How could he know I was his biggest fan ever? That I'd been inspired by *Cow-Cats & Aliens* to embrace a life of drama? That I'd traveled across the country to follow in his paw prints?

My hero didn't know me from Mittens.

So I made one of those life-changing decisions—I *would* find a way to make El Gato notice me. The time had come to climb every mountain, or at least the mountain of giant cardboard boxes stacked nearby. I

pulled myself up, higher and higher, box by box, until I reached the pinnacle. Then I stood as tall as one little Puffball can stand atop a stack of off-balance boxes. I spread my arms wide, cleared my throat, and called out to the greatest actor of this—or possibly any—century.

And that's when another unexpected thing happened. (If you read the last paragraph carefully and noted the term "off-balance," you may not be surprised. But I sure was.)

I LOVE YOU, EL GATO!

GROAN.

ALMOST THERE.

CAT NIP

THIS SIDE UP

THIS SIDE DOWN

DO NOT LEAN

PROPERTY OF PURRAMOUNT STUDIOS DO NOT CLIMB

GRUNT.

FRAGILE

FAKE CACTUS "U" BUILD IT

PETA APPROVED

FAUX FUR

Mr. Puffball stood on some boxes. Mr. Puffball had a great fall. All the king's horses and all the king's men didn't give a darn about me, lying on the floor with my fur askew. Yes, it hurt. Yes, it was embarrassing. Yes, there were those who called me crazy, loco, or just plain dumb. But El Gato was definitely looking at me now.

As a matter of fact, he kept his eyes locked on mine as he spoke to one of the studio cats. All I heard was "get," "crazy," "floor," and "perfect." Which I hoped was part of the sentence: "Get that crazy-talented cat off the floor because he would be perfect as my costar!"

The studio guy came over, helped me up, dusted me off, and said:

I managed a weak smile, because I didn't know a stunt cat from a grip and was still hoping he meant to say costar. But he said stunt cat, and he meant stunt cat. And I soon learned all about stunt cats, the hard way. Because when it comes to being a stunt cat, it's the hard way or the highway.

And I didn't even know how to drive.

EXPRESSION THAT SAYS, "YES I CAN."

THICK SKULL ELIMINATES NEED FOR HELMET.

SCAR FROM ALLIGATOR WRESTLING A NONPROFESSIONAL ALLIGATOR.

BIG MUSCLES FOR PUNCHING NEXT DIRECTOR WHO SAYS "BRING OUT THE ALLIGATOR!"

EXTRA-THICK CHEST FUR.

PANTS ARE FOR LOSERS.

STRIPE LOST TO RUNAWAY TRAIN SCENE GONE AWRY.

PROSTHETIC TAIL. REAL ONE DESTROYED DURING THE MOVIE ALLIGATORS A-GO-GO.

EXTRA-SHARP CLAWS FOR SLICING THROUGH DANGER.

STUNT CAT

BACKWARD BASEBALL CAP BECAUSE HE CAN.

SCAR FROM HEAD-CONKING, GIANT CAMERA. OW.

HEADSET FOR COMMUNICATING WITH DIRECTOR OR LISTENING TO GRIPPING MUSIC.

WALKIE-TALKIE FOR MESSAGES SUCH AS: "BEEF UP THE LIGHTS!" "THAT'S A WRAP!" OR "SOMEBODY GET ME A PROTEIN BAR!"

EXPRESSION THAT SAYS "YOU WANT LIGHTS WHERE? WHEN?! WHY?!"

I'M CREW

GLOVES FOR GRIPPING DOLLIES, HAND CRANES, AND PROTEIN BARS.

STEEL-TOE SHOES FOR UN-REASONABLE REQUESTS.

TOOL BELT FOR GAFFER TAPE, LASER POINTER, SCREW-DRIVERS, BUBBLE LEVEL, AND BUBBLE GUM.

GRIP

Bruiser

I was frog-marched out to the back lot, where there was a vast one-story building. Over it hung a sign:

DANGER!
STUNT CAT TRAINING AREA.
DANGER!

Under the sign stood the biggest cat I had ever seen. He was like four or five regular cats stacked on top of each other. He was so big I wasn't even sure he was a cat.

"Me Bruiser," he said.

"Hello, Bruiser," I said. "My name is Mr. Puffball, and I just fell off a mountain of boxes. Do you have an ice pack?"

"Fall good," said Bruiser. "Ice bad. You must tougher be."

BRUISER

REGULAR CATS

"I see your point," I said, "but my head is rather throbby. . . ."

Bruiser picked me up and hurled me into the air.

"TUCK! ROLL! No break neck if can."

I pictured myself landing via a graceful somersault. I thought of my time on my skateboard. That required grace. But this felt different. Because a huge "cat" had just hurled me across the room. I spun through the air with all the grace of a bowling ball in the gutter and smashed into the cement floor.

Oh, it was graceful. *NOT!*

"You must stunt cat!" said Bruiser. "Get into car and fast racing!"

If only I could have taken a power nap. Or had a refreshing glass of lemonade. Or hidden under a couch. But Bruiser was determined to force me into dangerous situations without telling me what to do.

That first day was hard. The second day was harder. The third day was equally hard. The fourth day was slightly less hard in the morning but way harder in the afternoon. And so on for the next two weeks.

Here are some of the phrases Bruiser enjoyed yelling at me:

"Ride bad-temper horse now! Going backward! Faster! Don't fall or you be trampled. See what I tell you?"

"We go to top of huge boulder so I push you off! Too much scraping and bleeding on boulder! Make body stronger!"

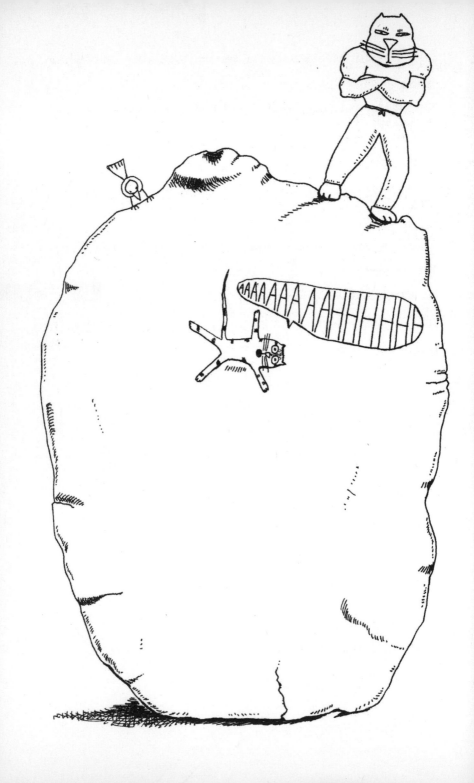

"I light tree on fire now and see how you jump from highest branch!"

"Rope climbing and swinging from tall pole do! Why let go of rope? You like hurt skull again?"

"Now we stand on top speeding train. Wind nice, refreshing, yes? Mr. Puffyball? Where you are?"

And here's what I would say:

"Ouch. Ouch. Ouchie. Ow. Could we take a break now, Bruiser? No? Ow. Please? Yeow! Arrrgghhh!!"

Okay, I'm exaggerating a little. Bruiser might be part cat. But it's a very small part. And he did hose me down once he realized the fireproof suit was not exactly fireproof. Never before has a cat so enjoyed being doused with water.

Plus, the afternoon sessions with Mei Wong, my kung fu teacher, were awesome.

Every evening, my old friends would help me through these hard times in their own way. Whiskers cracked me up with his hip-hop routine. Chet recounted his early days in Hollywood, when he was an actor in silent films and did his own stunts.

"That was before the days of 'No animals were harmed in the making of this movie,'" he said. "Good thing we have nine lives. I'm down to my last two."

Kitty sang showtunes while applying antiseptic and bandages to my cuts and bruises.

My friends called this part of my journey "paying my dues." And pay I did, day after day, scrape after scrape, bandage after bandage. But I went to sleep each night happy, knowing I'd soon be working alongside my hero, El Gato. And those two weeks really did transform me:

I was no longer Mr. Puffball (with no special words after my name).

I was Mr. Puffball, Stunt Cat to the Stars. And I was ready for anything.

Or was I?

BEFORE   AFTER

The Right Tuff

The day after I completed Stunt Cat Training with Bruiser, my new muscles and I sauntered over to Purramount Studios like we owned the place. Or at least had a temporary rental agreement.

The extras greeted me with a group "Wow!" They clearly thought stunt cats were way cool. Plus, I researched what qualifies as cool in Hollywood:

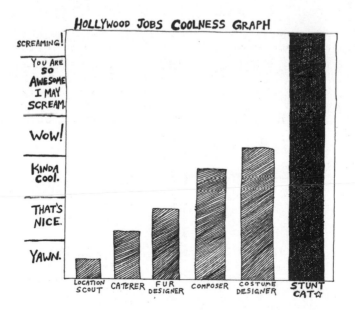

HOLLYWOOD JOBS COOLNESS GRAPH

Somebody handed me a description of the movie we were making:

NINE LIVES TO LIVE is a classic Western, with handsome heroes, sinister villains, and old-fashioned rattlesnakes. The setting is a small town, Tumbleweed, USA, back in the olden days, when sheriffs wore star-shaped badges and nobody took a shower, though a little cat-bath now and then wasn't unheard of. Where the good, the bad, and the ugly said things like, "Skedaddle, you varmint!" and "Whoa, Nellie!" and "There's a hoedown at the OK Corral!" Our main character is El Gato, a true tough guy, who comes to Tumbleweed with a thirst for revenge. El Gato is after Billy the Kitten, who square-danced with El Gato's one true love, Veronica, even though she prefers ballroom. After lots of rowdy fistfights, El Gato and his one true love are reunited. The movie ends with El Gato and Veronica finding Billy the Kitten holed up in a ghost town where even the ghosts dislike him. They steal Billy the Kitten's ten-gallon hat, which turns out to only hold five gallons. Laughing about their misadventure, El Gato and Veronica ride into the sunset, where they hope to open a hotel with a water slide.

Reading this made me even more revved up to start filming. I love Westerns! Plus I knew I would soon meet my hero, El Gato. But first I had to look like him. When I was thrown from a train or set on fire, the audience had to believe that the towering inferno of tabby onscreen was actually El Gato.

I stepped into the costume trailer.

"Here you go, Mr. Puffball," said the Costume Cat, dressing me in an authentic El Gato outfit. "I'll just straighten these hat pom-poms and . . . perfect."

My eyes nearly popped out of my head. This was miles away from the glitter and glue of my homemade costumes!

Now for the makeup—by none other than the fabulous Maybelline. She applied extra stripes and fur weaves and whisker extensions with an expert paw.

I thanked her and headed over to the filming locale. The day's set was a "desert" filled with fake cacti, sand flown in from Mexico, and tumbling tumbleweeds from Tumbleweeds 'R' Us. Surrounding all of this was a backdrop of painted mountains. And in the center stood a huge, real tree—the site of my first stunt.

I thought I'd die of happiness as Director DeMew yelled, "QUIET ON THE SET! PLACES, EVERYONE!" A majestic horse trotted out into the "desert" from Studio B. Then he—El Gato himself—strode over and said, "How goes it, Lightning?" and then shouted, "A little help!"

The director raised her megaphone and said, "Lights! Camera! Action!" And El Gato delivered the movie's epic opening line: "Giddyup!"

Lightning reared back with his flaxen mane gleaming in the sun. Now the star and his horse galloped around and around, while El Gato said:

"Run like the wind, Lightning!" and:

"Let's show those villains it's a bad day for villainy, Lightning!" and:

"Watch out for that gecko, Lightning!"

From out of nowhere came two of El Gato's nemeses, El Perro and Billy the Kitten, on horseback. They chased El Gato and Lightning straight toward the big tree, then rode off in opposite directions at the last moment. "Oh, no!" said El Gato. "That branch is really going to hurt!"

That was my cue.

"STUNT CAT!" shouted the director.

This was it. El Gato, Director DeMew, and all

those extras would watch me do my first cinematic stunt. My heart was pounding and my palms were sweaty. Plus, I wasn't used to wearing leather boots. My toes were even sweatier than my palms! I took a deep breath and walked over to El Gato, hoping he couldn't smell my fear (or my toes), and waited for him to dismount.

El Gato's eyes locked on mine. "Nobody rides Lightning but me. BRING OUT THUNDER!"

All at once the air filled with the sound of pounding hooves. Bruiser brought Thunder, the grouchy training horse, alongside me. He hopped off and said, "You have the right tuff, Mr. Puffyball. Be good now. Make Bruiser smiling."

"Thanks, Bruiser," I said, scrambling into the saddle. "I'll do my best."

Director DeMew said:

But Thunder didn't wait for "Action!" He bolted like he was running for the snack bar. My arms flailed as I grabbed for the reins, but it all happened so fast, in seconds I was wrapped around that branch like fettuccini on a fork.

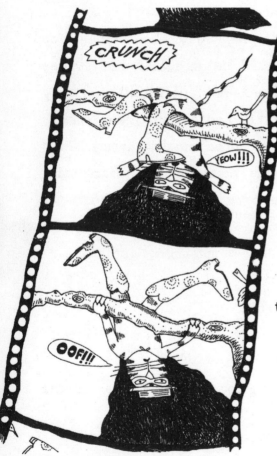

I spun like a kitten on a runaway carousel. The world flashed by in a crazy kaleidoscopic swirl. The air was knocked from my lungs. I heard Bruiser say, "Mr. Puffyball, is time to stop rotation." Finally, I was flung to the ground, where, through the magic of momentum, I somersaulted over and over again before crashing to a stop against a fake cactus with real needles. Ouch. I lay there, gasping for air and aching from ear to tail. What hurt the worst was my self-esteem. I'd made a fool of myself in front of everybody, including my lifelong hero. As I wallowed in my shame, two studio cats hoisted me up, dragged me off-camera, and yanked out the needles. Double ouch.

I expected Director DeMew to megaphone, "You call yourself a stunt cat?!" Instead, one of the extras yelled, "Good one, Mr. Puffball!" and they all cheered. I glanced over and saw Director DeMew not frowning, which was her way of saying "Good job!" Wow! They hadn't noticed that I didn't tuck and roll. They didn't care that I forgot to stay in character while spinning. All they saw was one *tuff* stunt cat.

Suddenly El Gato was right next to me. Which really took my breath away!

"That was not the worst thing I ever saw," he said.

"Thank you!"

"Kid, you're working for the biggest star in the world."

"Thank you!"

"And I should have the best stunt cat."

"Thank you!"

"I *had* the best stunt cat, but he sprained his tail on the first day. So now I'm stuck with you."

"Thank you!"

Director DeMew yelled, "El Gato—you're up!"

As El Gato turned to go, he added, "Next time, do better."

"Thank you!"

Then he yelled, "Maybelline, fix this kid's whiskers! They're not nearly as long and luxurious as mine."

"Thank you," I said as the extras whispered behind me.

I watched as El Gato walked back onto the set. I gasped quietly, realizing what had just happened. I couldn't believe it.

My hero had spoken to me.

A Series of Unfortunate Stunts

Over the next several months of filming, I stunted my tail off. Here are some of the highlights:

SCENE: EL GATO AND THE DEADLY SNAKES
Setting: A pit filled with poisonous snakes
El Gato's nemesis, El Perro, throws El Gato into a pit of poisonous snakes, saying, "Let's see you get out of this one, El Gato!" [Evil laugh!] Snakes writhe and wriggle all over El Gato, giving him the heebie-jeebies.

Of course they weren't really poisonous snakes. Except for the one El Gato planted there as a joke. When the snake told me he was poisonous, I leapt out of that pit faster than you can say "rattlesn—" El Gato has a great sense of humor!

SCENE: EL GATO AND THE EVIL FORTUNE TELLER

Setting: A fortune teller's tent

El Gato visits a fortune teller, who is actually his nemesis, Billy the Kitten, in disguise. Billy the Kitten says, "Close your eyes, El Gato, so I can smash you with this crystal ball—I mean, so I can read your future." El Gato closes his eyes and immediately gets conked on the head, big time. He collapses, then bounces back up for a round of fisticuffs.

The crystal ball was supposed to be papier-mâché. But El Gato felt it would be more realistic to use a glass ball. I could see his point. (I also saw stars!) That's show business for you.

SCENE: EL GATO IN THE HOT, HOT SUN
Setting: A deserted part of the desert

El Gato is tied to a wooden stake by another nemesis, Meanina, who says, "Adios, El Gato. I'd love to stay and watch you get the worst sunburn ever in this hot desert sun, but I have a dentist appointment." She rides off, laughing maniacally. Lightning rescues El Gato by chomping through the ropes, neighing, "Didn't I tell you to stay away from her?"

"EL GATO IN THE HOT, HOT SUN" TAKE TWELVE!

This was supposed to be a short scene that does not make your arms go numb. Except when you have to do twenty-nine takes. El Gato wanted to get it just right. He's a very serious actor!

SIGH.

SIGH.

SCENE: EL GATO AND THE EXPLODING FORT
Setting: The old fort

El Gato rushes into the old fort to rescue his one true love, Veronica, not realizing she has already escaped. He runs in, sees her exiting out the back door, and follows her. The moment he's out of danger, the fort goes blammo! El Gato looks back and says, "Not this time, Billy the Kitten."

In this kind of scene, timing is essential. The explosives expert was waiting for the exact safe moment to detonate the TNT. But El Gato chose the exact wrong moment to use the detonator as a footstool.

ACME
TNT
DETONATOR

So instead of:

1. Rush into fort
2. Rush out of fort
3. *Blammo!*

. . . it was:

1. Rush into fort
2. *Blammo!*

Like I said, timing is essential.

SCENE: EL GATO AND THE
DANGEROUS CHASM
Setting: A rope bridge over an incredibly
deep chasm
El Gato races across a wobbly rope bridge
and reaches the other side seconds before
it is cut down by Meanina.

The essential issue was that El Gato should not
have slapped me on the back while I was leaning over
the chasm. Fortunately, I only smacked into two jutting rocks before landing in the net. Not bad!

SCENE: EL GATO AND THE CRUEL SHARK

Setting: A room with a shark tank

I'd rather not go into it. Let's just say sharks are not my friends.

At least he was a professional, unlike that alligator El Gato invited to lunch.

Then there was the quicksand prank. Hilarious!

One evening, I was home with the gang when Chet asked, "So how's our old friend El Gato?"

"You know El Gato?" I asked.

Chet chuckled. "Oh, El Gato and I go way back."

"That kitten could not sing," said Kitty.

"And he had no sense of rhythm," said Whiskers. "Though he tried to salsa all over the studio."

"Sounds messy," I said. "But when did you meet him?"

"Meet him?" said Chet, whipping out an old poster. "Why, I gave that fat cat his first big break in the movies. We called him El Gatito."

"He looks different," I said.

"Of course he looks different," said Chet. "He was just an itty-bitty kitty."

"I wonder why he never visits," I said.

"Guess he's too important for old friends," said Chet. "Anyway, how do you like working with the great and powerful El Gato?"

"He's a great actor."

Chet picked some lint off his sweater, then raised his eyes to mine and said, "But not such a great cat?"

I admitted that working with El Gato wasn't always easy. Sometimes he was grouchy. The littlest thing could set him off.

"He does have an excellent sense of humor," I said, and told them about the quicksand prank. "I was licking sand out of my fur for days. Isn't that hysterical?"

"Nope," said Ms. Kitty.

"Absolutely not," said Whiskers.

"I'll quicksand him!" said Chet, shaking his fist.

"You don't get it," I said. "El Gato is my hero. He even invited me out to the Brown Tabby tonight. I told him about you guys, and you're all invited, too!"

"Why?" said Chet.

"El Gato said he has a special job for us. Maybe he wants to do another movie together."

"The Brown Tabby—our old hangout!" said Kitty.

"I'll slip into my dancing pants," said Whiskers.

"I'll fluff my fur," said Kitty.

"I'll pick more lint off my sweater," said Chet. "And I'm gonna tell that cat *ixnay on the ickquay andsay.*"

"Forget it," I said. "Let's just have fun. El Gato's picking us up in his limousine. He said to listen for his horn, which plays . . ."

114

"Leaping lizards!" cried Chet.

Whiskers mamboed back into the room. "Kitty, Chet, let's show these youngsters how to shake it!" And he danced us all out the door.

Limo Scene

We all piled into El Gato's limousine. The fur-lined interior had everything from cup holders and catnip to a climbing wall and a mini fridge.

But the first few moments inside were not as warm and fuzzy as the seats. I worried how my old friends and El Gato would get along. Not too good, from the looks of things. Chet jabbed at his car pillow, saying, "I hate sequins!" Kitty sang, "I'm bad, I'm bad, I'm a bad, bad cat . . ." and Whiskers' dancing feet

kicked one of the cup holders and snapped it in half. I sneezed to break the tension but it didn't make a dent.

Finally El Gato said, "Your friends are old and weird, Stunt Cat."

Chet glared at him. "His name is Mr. Puffball. And we're not old."

"Sure," chuckled El Gato. "You're not old like I'm not famous." He reached into the mini fridge for a glass of chilled milk.

"Once, you wouldn't have been so rude," said Chet.

El Gato took a long sip, his eyes locked on Chet. He finished sipping and said, "Do I know you?"

Chet's fur stood on end. I'd never seen him so angry. "Know me? I gave you your first break, Gatito!"

El Gato slammed his glass into the cup holder. "What did you call me?!"

GATITO.
GATITO.
GATITO.
GATITO.
GATITO!

El Gato let out a low hiss and activated his claws. "I am EL GATO."

Chet hissed back and raised his cane. "I am not old."

"Hey, buddies," I said, "let's calmly talk about making a movie together. How about *Dogzilla*—with cats? *Catzilla*!" Sadly, my excellent idea was drowned out by the hissing.

Kitty whipped out her kazoo and played the theme song from *A Tail of Two Kitties*. El Gato's ears swiveled toward her. His whiskers twitched, and his claws retracted. "Well, well, well, if it isn't Lester B. Rumpus the Fifth and you other cats."

"Chester P. Grumpus the Third, Kitty LaRue, and Whiskers!" said Chet.

"Whatev," said El Gato. "As you see, old director from my past, I am now a humongous star, and you are wearing a linty sweater. But tonight's your lucky night. Because tonight your job is . . ." El Gato wiped at his milk moustache with the back of his paw. ". . . to keep me constantly amused. I must never be hungry, sleepy, or visited by fleas. I dub you all my— wait for it—*Entourage!* And you, Stunt Cat, have the extra task of guarding my fabulous whiskers."

Chet put on a scowl to rival Grumpy Cat. Whiskers asked if we were on a reality show.

"The reality," said El Gato, "is you get to hang out with a famous movie star."

Chet slapped his paws against his bony knees. "Whiskers and Kitty are famous movie stars! Why, back in the day . . ."

"*BORING!*" interrupted El Gato. "New topic. I got you, my *Entourage*, awesome presents." And he handed us each one of these:

"Interesting," said Kitty.

"Sparkling," said Whiskers.

"I don't wear necklaces," said Chet.

I gave him a meaningful look and said, "C'mon, Chet. It'll be like we're in a club."

"*Entourage*," said El Gato as the limo pulled to a stop.

Whiskers, Kitty, and I put on our bling, and I forced Chet's over his big head. Then we followed El Gato into the Brown Tabby.

As soon as I stepped inside, I gasped. Dozens of familiar faces stared at me. With another gasp, I realized they were photos of my favorite movie stars. Next to them was a jaw-dropping assortment of movie treasures.

Wow! It was like stepping into a movie lover's dream. Except I didn't have my pillow or tiny El Gato. I turned and saw the Catmobile parked in one corner of the room. To my left was a life-size statue of a well-dressed cat. *Must be from Madame Twoclaw's Wax Museum*, I thought, poking it firmly. *Probably a replica of a famous butler from one of those mystery movies where they say, "The butler did it."*

RAPUNZEL'S EXTENSION

EVERLASTING GOBSTOPPER

LUKE'S LIGHTEST SABER

BRIDE OF FRANKENSTEIN'S WIG

THE BLOB

JACK SPARROW'S COMPASS

HAIRY PAWTER'S READING GLASSES

FRANKENSTEIN'S NECK SCREWS

JACK SKELLINGTON'S LEFT FEMUR

THE LORAX'S MOUSTACHE

BILBO'S 'STING'

FAIRY DUST

TOM THUMB'S THUMBPRINT

THE CIRCLE OF LIFE

UF○

CROOK-SHANKS'S FUR

DO NOT EAT! OLAF'S NOSE

LION KING'S THEME

F.MR. FOX TAIL

SPIDERCAT'S FIRST WEB

KERMIT'S BANJO

SON OF DRACULA'S BABY FANGS

SPONGEBOB'S SQUAREPANTS

TINKER'S BELL

SNOW WHITE'S APPLE

UNKNOWN STAR

FLYING BROOMSTICK OF THE WICKED WITCH OF THE WEST

Or it could have been a waiter. Actually, he was a waiter. I knew it as soon as he said,

As we followed the waiter and El Gato, I had a feeling the fun was just beginning.

Or was it?

Dancing with the Star

The waiter led us to a table in a ballroom filled with fancy Hollywood cats. In the center of the room was a fish tank as big as New Jersey. Seeing all those tropical fish swimming gracefully through the water made my tummy rumble audibly. The aroma from a huge platter of fish tacos only made my hungry noises noisier.

El Gato pulled the platter toward himself and wasted no time in stuffing his face but good. And that's when I learned the true meaning of "see-food."

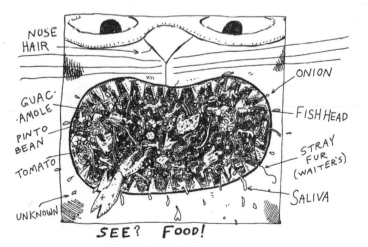

NOSE HAIR

ONION

GUAC-AMOLE

FISH HEAD

PINTO BEAN

STRAY FUR (WAITER'S)

TOMATO

SALIVA

UNKNOWN

SEE? FOOD!

Chomp, crunch, swallow. "Best fish tacos ever!"

"They sure look yummy," said Whiskers, a line of drool escaping down his chin.

"And they smell delicious," said Kitty, licking her lips.

"I like tacos," said Chet, showing his yellow teeth.

El Gato lunged protectively toward his food. Then he noticed the whole restaurant watching and announced, "Fish tacos for my *Entourage*, waiter!"

Soon our table was covered in platters. What can I say about those amazing fish tacos?

There was still several meals' worth of tacos left when El Gato raised his head and yelled, "DESSERT!" The waiter rushed over and placed a gigantic anchovy-covered cheesecake in the middle of our table. We devoured it in seconds. Without forks! Then El Gato said, "TOYS! NOW!"

"Very good, sir," said the waiter. "You will be pleased to hear that tonight is Wacky String Night."

"That is pleasing," said El Gato.

The waiter clapped his hands twice. Another waiter hurried over with a tray holding five cans of Wacky String. It's string that you spray. In other words, the best thing ever!! We each got one can, and El Gato was given a disposable camera, which he handed to me, saying, "You take the pictures."

El Gato grabbed his Wacky String and jumped up. "Let the String Games begin; may the odds be ever in your favor!"

Whiskers fought valiantly. Kitty used hers stylishly. Chet kept saying, "How does this contraption work?" I was spraying and snapping pics like a pro. It was every fun thing I could imagine rolled into one: celebrities, friends, and string!

EL GATO'S SNEAK ATTACK.

WHISKER'S COUNTERATTACK.

KITTY'S WACKY DO!

CHET, CONFUSED.

But then El Gato ran out of Wacky String. Shaking the can repeatedly, he announced, "This is no longer making me happy." He looked around and spotted me. "Stunt Cat, go tell the Catnip 'n' Things lady I want more Wacky String."

"Sure thing," I said, spraying him with the last of my string. He laughed and tossed his empty can at me. It bounced off my head and squirted its last squirt into my eye. Ow. Wow. My hero, El Gato, and I, Mr. Puffball, were playing together like old friends. Best night ever!

As I ran over to the Catnip 'n' Things cat, my foot caught on some string. I went sailing through the air, grabbed a chair back, and did a flip before crashing into her. She dropped her Catnip 'n' Things tray and instantly transformed into Kung Fu Kitty. Instinctively, I did the same. As she was about to deliver a killer chop, I recognized her dauntless stance and said, "A fellow student of Mei Wong, I see." We bowed to each other and laughed.

"Sorry about that!" she said, picking up her tray.

"No prob," I said.

"Catnip?"

"They call me Mr. Puffball, Stunt Cat to the Stars."

"I'm Rosie," she said. "And I know your name's not
Catnip. I meant, do you want some catnip?"

"I knew that," I said, chuckling. "No, thanks, but I
do need more Wacky String for none other than—wait
for it—El Gato."

"No can do," she said.
"That troublemaker is on
a one-can limit. The last
time we gave him extra
Wacky String, we
almost lost a
waiter."

VERY GOOD, SIR.

127

I explained that I was part of El Gato's entourage and contractually obligated to keep him amused at all times. Rosie was unimpressed by my use of the phrase *contractually obligated* and refused to give me any more string. She suggested I go back to El Gato and do the bad news/good news routine. The bad news: they were out of string (not true). The good news: the Retro-Swing-Dance Contest was about to start (true).

"Would you do that for me, Mr. Puffball? You know El Gato can't resist a contest."

I looked into her big green eyes and imagined saying, "I'd do anything for you, baby." But what I actually said was—"Okey dokey." Then I left, glancing back at Rosie with a leading-man kind of look. I attempted a wink but accidentally closed both eyes, which made me trip again. I rolled into an awkward somersault but sprang up kung-fu-style next to El Gato, who said, "Cool it, Stunt Cat. Where's my Wacky String?"

Fortunately, I was saved from answering by the sudden swell of music. My starstruck eyes were shocked to see that onstage stood the world famous pop star Tabby Gaga.

"Gaga," I muttered. "Dance contest."

"Dance contest?!" said Whiskers and El Gato at the same time.

Whiskers grabbed Kitty's hand, and El Gato grabbed a nearby glamour-puss, and off they twirled to the dance floor. Now I was on duty as: Whisker Guard to the Star. I moved next to El Gato and shadowed his every step, making sure nobody disturbed his luxuriously long whiskers. It wasn't easy. His dancing could best be described as "crazy-style."

129

It involved lots of kicking, bouncing, and throwing his partner.

And then there were Whiskers and Kitty. They were so graceful, they were waltzing the pants off El Gato. And he wasn't even wearing pants.

I feared the dance contest would not end well. Because I'd been around El Gato enough to know his likes and dislikes. I made a quick mental list of these and called it:

EL GATO'S LIKES AND DISLIKES

Likes	Dislikes
1. Himself	1. Not being the best at
2. His limo	something
3. His fish tacos	

If El Gato did not win this dance contest, he would not be happy. Maybe he would cry. Or disband his entourage. Or bite whoever was closest to him (me!).

The music stopped abruptly, and Tabby Gaga said, "The judge has chosen a winner."

"Excellent," said El Gato, dropping his dance partner to the floor and sticking out his chest. "I am ready for my Medal of Bestness."

But the judge walked right past El Gato, straight to Whiskers and Kitty. "Congratulations!" she said, handing them a trophy.

"Thank you," said Kitty. "And now for one final dip." But before the dipping even began, we all heard a loud *whoosh*!

El Gato had tossed his tacos!

"Gatito!" said Kitty. "Calm down!"

But he did not calm down. Leaping from table to table, he stomped, roared, and broke everything in his path.

Then he raced out to the lobby and came back clutching the Wicked Witch of the West's broom.

"Please, sir," said the waiter. "Put down the broom."

But El Gato did not put it down. He jumped onstage, mounted the broom, took a running start, and soared toward the musicians' pit, yowling, "I'm flying!" We covered our ears as trumpets and piccolos smashed into cymbals and kettledrums. Then El Gato came crashing through the antique harp, yelling, "I am not amused!!"

He climbed up to the rim of the fish tank. Just as he was poised to dive in, the police showed up and yelled, "Stop! You know you can't swim, El Gato. Get down here."

El Gato bowed his head like a kitten who'd been given a time-out, slid down, and left with the police. Rosie walked up to me and said, "I told you that cat was trouble." Then Maybelline appeared out of nowhere and tapped me on the shoulder. "El Gato really destroyed the place this time. You know what that means, Mr. Puffball?"

"The janitors have to work later than usual?"

"And El Gato is going to anger management class. The district judge said he'd have to if he lost his cool again, and he certainly lost it tonight."

"But El Gato has his big love scene tomorrow," I said.

"Yes," said Maybelline, "the big love scene *must* be filmed tomorrow. Otherwise we'll go over budget, and we've already spent a million dollars on this movie!"

"But then who's going to . . ." And that's when I saw everybody pointing at me. "But won't El Gato be angry when he finds out I did his scene while he was in anger management class?"

Chet put his paw on my shoulder. "He won't be angry. He'll be punchy."

"Anybody else have an opinion?"

They answered me with pitying looks, like they feared my nine lives to live would soon be used up— which made me fear I might toss my tacos.

Hiss? Kiss!

I know what you're thinking:

What's the big deal? You've been El Gato in a pit of deadly snakes, falling into an incredibly deep chasm, and wrestling a non-union shark.

But this was different. Why was it different? Let me explain:

STUNT CAT

- A stunt cat wears an **El Gato outfit.**
- A stunt cat **groans with** pain.
- A stunt cat knows El Gato wants to avoid those scenes where he's **thrown from a train.**

UNDERSTUDY

- An understudy wears **El Gato's actual outfit.**
- An understudy **groans with** disappointment if there's no caviar at the buffet.
- An understudy knows when El Gato finds out he did his big scene he might be **thrown from a train.** By El Gato.

And yet, if I truly wanted to be an actor, I had to seize this opportunity to act like my favorite actor. So I went to Purramount Studios the next day.

When I arrived, I looked around to make sure El Gato had not returned from anger management class. Because if he saw me stealing his big scene, he might start smashing things again, such as my ears. Next I snuck into El Gato's trailer. The costume designer dressed me. Maybelline striped and whiskered me. "Good luck," they said as I left. "You'll need it."

I strode onto the set, hoping I could pass as the real El Gato.

Director DeMew stared at me for a long time. Then she said, "Have you ever acted before, kid?"

"Well, I am a stunt—"

"Don't interrupt! Look, kid, do you know how many cats dream of a chance like this?"

"Not offhand," I said, "but maybe if you lend me a calculator . . ."

"Quiet! Yesterday, you were Mr. Puffball, Stunt Cat to the Stars," she said. "But today you are El Gato, the Star. You've got to think like El Gato, talk like El Gato, and burp like El Gato. Dosh garn it, you've got to *be* El Gato! Can you do that, *EL GATO?*"

I pointed to myself and raised my eyebrows to make sure she meant me, even though she'd said "El Gato." Director DeMew mouthed, *Yes, you!*

"I think so," I murmured.

She picked up her megaphone: "I CAN'T HEAR YOU!"

As the ringing in my ears subsided, I thought about Chet, Whiskers, and Kitty and how hard they worked, teaching me to be a triple threat. I thought of my mother, who believed in me when no one else did. I thought about how excellent I look in a black cape. Then I threw back my shoulders and said, "Yes, Director DeMew, I can do that!"

And that's when she said:

"You mean someone else is in this scene?" I asked.

"That's the plan. Unless you want to do the big love scene by yourself."

I turned and saw a she-cat gliding toward me. I nodded as if to say, "Welcome, Ms. Costar. Nothing to worry about here. It's only me, El Gato." Then she lifted her veil. And that's when I almost soiled my cape. Because I was about to do a big Hollywood love scene with Tabby Gaga!

My confidence melted away like a snowman in Florida. I got sweaty all over. Worst of all, I flubbed my lines. A lot!

I was losing hope. But then I asked myself, "What would El Gato do?" I straightened my pom-poms, took a deep breath, and said, "I think I've got it now."

"Oh, joy," said Director DeMew. She was so encouraging!

Perfect at last! I took a deep but modest bow and said, "I guess we're done here."

"Not quite, *El Gato*," said Director DeMew. "Read the script!"

"But I already recited all my lines. There is a stage direction that says *Hiss*, but why would I hiss at my one true love?"

"Kiss!" said Director DeMew. "Kiss!"

I held up one paw. "No kiss needed, Director. I'm just doing my job."

The Director picked up her megaphone and marched toward me, making angry director noises. My paws were stuck in my ears, but I still heard her quite clearly: "Kiss her!!"

My stomach squeezed shut. I, the Actor Formerly Known as Stunt Cat, was supposed to kiss one of the most famous cats in the world!

"You know how to kiss, don't you?" purred Tabby Gaga. "Just put your lips together and press your furry face against mine."

I tried to chuckle in a manly way, but it came out more like a gagging cough. "Sure, I know. I'm what you might call a kissing expert."

"Then come here, tiger," she said.

"Is there a tiger in this scene?" I asked, glancing around. "I thought I was done with all my stunts."

But I was not done. Because now I had to do the scariest stunt of all: kissing a celebrity without drooling, making inappropriate noises, or accidentally smooching her nose.

So I asked myself, "What would Mr. Puffball do?" Because it was Mr. Puffball who had brought me to this moment. *That took courage*, I thought, *traveling across the country, performing for the hobos of Hobowood, training with Bruiser, carrying out perilous stunts.* Many were the times I could have turned back. But I didn't.

And I wasn't about to turn back now.

"Let's do this thing, tiger or no tiger," I said, stepping close to Tabby Gaga. She turned her face up, and I smelled French perfume mixed with anchovies. And in that moment I discovered my inner kissing expert.

TV! Flying! Peanuts!

Early the next morning, I was startled awake by the sound of loud rock music: *"We are the champions . . ."*

El Gato's limo! What if he was back and madder than ever? I hid deep inside my blankies. But the song played on, and there wasn't a blankie in the world that could protect me. I knew I had to rise and face the limo horn.

Plus, Chet repeatedly poked me with his cane, yelling, "That noise is making my hearing aid whistle! *Do the Right Thing* and make it stop!" For an old guy, he's got a mighty strong jab. So when I peeked out and saw his cane poised for another strike, I got up.

As a precaution, I placed a paper bag over my head. Then I grabbed tiny El Gato for luck and slowly stuck my head outside. Anyone looking would think an innocent paper bag had simply floated out the front door.

The limo was there, but the good news was: *No El Gato!* Sitting in the backseat was Tabby Gaga, alone, in her *Nine Lives to Live* outfit.

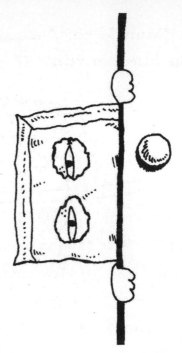

"What are you doing here, Ms. Gaga?" I asked.

"Why are you wearing a paper bag over your head?" she asked.

"I haven't shaved yet," I said, in a manly voice. I wasn't ready to expose myself. "So what are you doing here, Ms. Gaga?"

"I'm picking you up for our day of media events," she said, handing me El Gato's clothes. "Put these on."

I raced inside, dressed, put on whisker extensions, and restriped. Then I swaggered my way back to the limo. I got inside, unsure whether she knew my secret identity. So I twitched my whiskers and asked, "Do you know who I am?"

"You're El Gato," she said. "And I'm Tabby Gaga."
She lifted her veil.

Gasp! She wasn't Tabby Gaga. She was the Catnip
'n' Things girl from the Brown Tabby. "Rosie! Why
are you impersonating Tabby Gaga? Is she in anger
management class, too?"

Rosie explained that Tabby Gaga hated doing media
events. "She asked me to take her place, so here I am.
Now let's raid the mini fridge!"

We pigged out but good. After some belly patting
and momentous burping, Rosie said, "Any questions
about our day of media events?"

"Only one. What's a media event?"

In case you didn't know either, media events are what movie stars do to whip up a frenzy of anticipation about their movies. We had to make cats everywhere believe that *Nine Lives to Live* would be . . .

THE MUST-SEE MOVIE of THE YEAR!

. . . coming soon to a theater near you!

This was our whirlwind schedule for the day:

MEDIA EVENTS AGENDA
FOR NINE LIVES TO LIVE

6:00 A.M. TV interview by J. Meow on *Good Morning, Hollywood!*

7:00 Photo op with the governor of California, Arnold Katzenjammer

ARNOLD KATZENJAMMER USED TO BE AN ACTOR, TOO!

8:00 Pawprints in front of Furman's Chinese Theater
9:00 Brunch at Mr. Chow's Silver Bowl, followed by photo shoot with the photographer from *Cats Who Brunch* magazine

THE LOBSTER WAS SO GREAT, WE ORDERED TOFU INSTEAD!

3:30 Arrive in New York City for a mix 'n' meow at Catz's Deli

SHE-CAT LIBERTY: THANK YOU, FRANCE!

4:30 Meet with journalists from various magazines and newspapers

THE JOURNALISTS ASKED SO MANY QUESTIONS!

6:00 Relax on the plane ride back to Hollywood. You're done! Good job!

By the end of that glorious day, I felt like the luckiest cat in the world. Rosie was more fun than Tabby

ROSIE + I WENT ALL NUTTY ON THE FLIGHT HOME.

Gaga and tougher than Governor Katzenjammer. She planted her paws into the wet cement in front of Furman's Chinese Theater without one "Ew." And she was kind. When the lobster told her how he'd been treated at Mr. Chow's Silver Bowl, she took him home to live with her. And she wasn't even planning to eat him!

I was pooped by the time the limo brought me back to MGM. But I had lived one day like a real star—wined, dined, and photographed with my new best friend, Rosie. Nothing could have made me lose my smile right then.

Until I saw Chet. "I'm surprised you can still smile when you know El Gato is back from anger management class," he said. "Or didn't you know? I bet his anger did not manage very well."

The Nightmare
Before Trickiness

I was back in New York City.

Rosie and I were waltzing on the Empire State Building's observation deck when we observed something bubbling up from the reservoir in Central Park. Huge ears broke the dark surface, followed by a humongous, angry El Gato. With a terrible yowl, he stomped down Fifth Avenue, straight toward us.

"Get me my dancing pants," said Whiskers. "I'm gonna moonwalk this creature back to his black lagoon."

Then fifty-foot El Gato loomed over us, roaring, "STUNT CAT, YOU STOLE MY SCENE!" He grabbed me with one limo-size paw and climbed up to the top of the spire.

El Gato–Kong beat his chest with the hand I rested in. It was not restful. Flying lobsters circled his head, flaming the fire of his fury. He swiped at them and dropped me.

And I was falling, falling, falling through lobster-filled skies.

"Get up," said Rosie.

"I can't," I whispered. "I'm falling."

"Up," she repeated, jabbing me with her cane. Her voice sounded gravelly. "Wake up, *Sleeping Beauty*!"

"Wha . . ." I pried one eye open. I wasn't in New York, and there was no giant El Gato. It had all been a crazy dream. Chet stood over me, glaring down with a look that said, *Get up, face your fears, and* return *El Gato's clothes. But iron them first. They're wrinkly.*

I stared back with a look that said, *All right, I'll get up. But nobody can make me iron.*

Chet was right. I'd have to face El Gato eventually. And who knew? Maybe everything would be okay. Maybe El Gato was happy I'd stepped in and saved the film from going over budget. Maybe he'd give me a hug and say, "I heard you kissed Tabby Gaga. You rock!" Or maybe he'd say, "I heard you stole my scene. You stink!" And I'd run away as he pursued me with intent to punch. Either way, I had to face my destiny, be it huggy or be it punchy.

"Here," said Whiskers, handing me a breakfast burrito as I walked into the kitchen. It had *Good Luck* written on it in hot sauce.

"Thanks," I said, gobbling it down.

Then Kitty handed me an embroidered handkerchief.

"For good luck?" I asked.

"To stop the bleeding," she said.

Chet held out my old sash and tiny El Gato. "Maybe this will help him remember the cuddly Gatito within."

"Thanks," I said, "but I'll be fine. El Gato is still my hero."

"Of course you'll be fine," said Whiskers, sniffling.

My old friends walked me to the door and waved good-bye, the sunlight glinting off their tear-filled eyes.

I turned, took a deep breath, and set off. I was wearing El Gato's clothes so he'd see how much I wanted to be like him. Soon I was at Purramount Studios.

"El Gato!" said one of the grips as I stepped inside. "I thought you said you'd be gone all day at the Celebrity Cat Spa?"

"Yes," I said, twitching my whiskers. "I, El Gato, will be gone. But I, El Gato, am here now because I . . . forgot my fluffy towel! So would you carry me to my dressing room, please?"

"Sure thing," said the grip, picking me up. "I never heard you say please before."

"Well, now it pleases me to say please, and I'll say please whenever I please."

"Sounds like a plan." He put me down in front of El Gato's dressing room.

"El Gato has many plans," I said, pretending to search for my dressing room key as the grip walked away. If I could get inside, I could return El Gato's clothes and go home unharmed. But of course I did not have a key. So I tried the door handle.

Locked.

I jiggled the handle and pushed with all my strength. *Jiggle, push! Jiggle, push, PUSH!* Nothing. *Quiet groan.* Then I remembered the words of my kung fu master, Mei Wong: "Use the force, Mr. Puffball."

Or was it "Use the forks"? I didn't have any forks with me, so I decided to go with force. I closed my eyes and used the force of an awesome kung fu kick.

I stepped inside and closed the door. Then I turned around and— *Wow!*

Looking at all those amazing costumes roused a special feeling inside me, and I knew there was something I had to do: TRY THEM ON! So I did. Each costume change was like a page in the book *El Gato's Greatest Cinematic Moments*. If there were such a book.

① AN AMERICAN PURRSIDENT ② *HAIRY PAWTER AND THE GOBLET OF FUR!* ③ *MEWTINY ON THE BOUNTY* ④ *PLAN FELINE FROM OUTER SPACE.* ⑤ *LA CAT AUX FOLLES*

Finally, I put on El Gato's signature outfit, for one last hurrah before heading home. The moment I tried on the genuine Corinthian leather cape, I heard someone turn the door handle and say, "Why is there a pawprint on my door?" I quickly dove behind the vanity, knocking out the mirror in the process. One second later, El Gato came in.

All the costumes were neatly hung back in the closet. The mirror had fallen out in one piece and rolled beside me, so no broken glass. Nothing appeared amiss as El Gato sat down at his vanity. He looked into the "mirror," and this is what he saw:

And I thought, *If I'm twice the actor I think I am, I might just get away with this.*

Mirror, Mirror

What got me through the next fur-raising scene was the very thing that had gotten me into this situation in the first place: I was El Gato's biggest fan. I'd been obsessively studying his every move for months. I knew his habits. I knew his expressions. I knew how many times a day he visited the litter box. I was ready to be his mirror.

So when he tilted his head back to check for nose hairs, so did I.

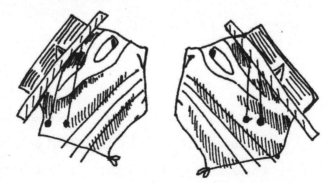

When he washed his ears, so did I.

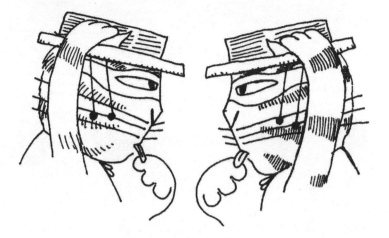

When he turned around for an over-the-shoulder glance, so did I.

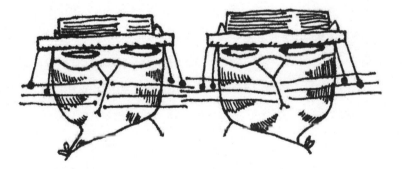

And when he started in with the whisker grooming, so did I. Only he didn't stop. He smoothed and fussed with those whiskers for what felt like an eternity.

Was I witnessing El Gato's secret to luxuriously long whiskers? Or was one of those things that you don't expect to happen about to happen? Either way, I was getting nervous. El Gato's whiskers may have been real (note the "may have been"), but mine were not. I'd already spent two days wearing those whisker extensions. They'd been slept on, sneezed on, and immersed in soup. They wouldn't hold out much longer. But if I didn't mirror his movements exactly, I would be discovered, which might lead to my tragic ending. So I twirled and smoothed and fussed with those whiskers until, of course, they popped right off!

But guess what? So did El Gato's! In terms of my mirror trick, this should have been good news. But I turned it into bad news by gasping. Loudly.

"YOU!" said El Gato.

"You!" I echoed, in a desperate attempt to continue
my trickery.

"Enough!" said El Gato.

Scrambling out from behind the vanity, I sput-
tered, "Sorry, Gatito, Tito, El Ito . . ." Meanwhile,

El Gato was turning a shade of red I didn't think possible for a tabby. His fur stood on end and out came the claws. But I only saw this in my peripheral vision, because I could not tear my eyes away from those tiny, tiny whiskers.

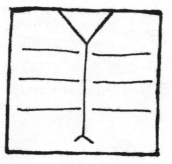

I blurted out, "Tiny whiskers." Then it was like the world stood still, with El Gato frozen in attack mode. I held my breath, waiting for claws to strike me. Instead, his fur deflated and his claws retracted. His arms fell to his sides, and he whispered these words: *"Calmness . . . is . . . me."*

"Excuse me?" I said.

"Calmness is me," he said, his shoulders slumping. "That's what they taught us in anger management class."

"Did they clip your whiskers, too?" I asked.

He looked confused for a moment. "YES!" he said

at last. "Yes, yes, yes. Those evil cats clipped my whiskers. And now I'm forced to use extensions, just like you."

"How awful!" I said.

"Isn't it awful?" said El Gato, putting an arm around my shoulders. "And you know what would be even more awful?"

"If they took your limo?"

"No!" said El Gato. "*Calmness is me.* What would be even more awful is if my fans found out. What a

terrible blow for little Snowball and little Cupcake and little Ginger. If my fans found out about my whiskers, it would ruin me. I mean, them."

"I'm sure your fans would still love you," I said. "I do."

"But," said El Gato. "*Calmness*. My fans might lash out against those cats who clipped my whiskers. They might even cause a riot, right here in Hollywood. All because YOU told someone about my whiskers. We don't want to start a riot, do we?"

He shook his head and so did I, and we both said, "Noooo."

"So let's keep this whole"—he mouthed the words *whiskers thing*—"a secret. Mr. Puckball can keep a secret for his old pal El Gato, right?"

"Mr. Puffball," I said. "And yes, I can. . . ."

But then I noticed he was staring at tiny El Gato, who was still tied around my waist.

"You really like me, don't you?" he said.

"You're my hero! My mother gave me this after I saw *Cow-Cats & Aliens* and decided to become an actor, just like you." I handed him tiny El Gato.

"Well, well," said El Gato. "A collectible El Gato doll. I always wished I'd gotten one for myself."

And then I said the words I never thought I'd utter: "Keep it. I don't need it anymore. I'm friends with the real El Gato."

"So you are," said El Gato. "Tell you what, Mr. Fuzzball. I'm going back to the Brown Tabby tonight to show the world I can be as calm as the next cat. Why don't you and your old friends come along?"

"As your entourage?" I asked. "It's Puffball, by the way."

"No," said El Gato, giving me a squeeze. "As my friends."

"We'd love to!" I said. "I only wish I had something new to wear."

"Your wish is my command, Mr. Fluffball, my secret-keeping friend." El Gato opened a drawer, rummaged around, and handed me this—

"Awesome! Thank you. And it's Mr. Puffball." I took off El Gato's outfit and put on my new bow tie.

"Now you look like a modern Hollywood star, *Mr. Puffball*," said El Gato. "And remember"—he mouthed the words *Don't tell ANYONE about my WHISKERS or you will start a RIOT.*

And I gave El Gato a look that said, *Your secret is safe with me, pal.*

The Desolation of
Mr. Puffball

When El Gato picked us up that evening, his limo horn did not play "We Are the Champions." Instead, we heard El Gato's voice chanting "calmness is me" on an endless loop.

"What the what?" said Chet.

"It's the new calm El Gato," I said, straightening my bow tie. "You're gonna love him."

"If we get more fish tacos, I love him already," said Whiskers.

"Even if he does sing like a bloodhound with a head cold," said Kitty.

"As long as I don't have to wear a necklace, I'm in," said Chet.

"Then let's go!" I said.

The limo ride went as calmly as could be expected, and soon we were all back at the Brown Tabby.

The moment we entered the ballroom, Rosie cast me an uneasy look. I strolled over. "No worries, Rosie. El Gato is chill. You should get to know him, because we're best friends now, and I will probably be costarring in his next movie."

"Well," she told me, "I've been brushing up on my kung fu just in case."

"Excellent," I said, "but that won't be necessary." As I moseyed back to our table, I saw a sudden flash of bright blue wig. Tabby Gaga was onstage again.

"Hey, you crazy cats," she said, "time to go wild to some paw-stomping tunes! *ONE, TWO, THREE, FOUR . . .*"

"This is my kind of music!" said El Gato. He turned to a nearby she-cat, bowed, and asked, "Would you care to join me on the dance floor?"

Kitty turned to Whiskers. "Let's rock!"

Even Chet found a dance partner, and so did I. Soon I was in my happy place—bopping with Rosie and listening to awesome music, surrounded by good friends. Watching Whiskers and Kitty doing their old-time dances only magnified my smile:

It was all good. That is, until Whiskers and Kitty did the mashed potato—a dance that involves the following steps:

1. Put your hands in the air.
2. Pretend your hands are potatoes.
3. Mash.

If only there had been a step between 2 and 3 that said:

2½. Make sure you have not accidentally grabbed the whisker extensions of a nearby cat who is prone to temper tantrums.

All would have continued being good. But they left out that crucial step. So this happened:

We all heard a *RIP!* followed by the sound of Whiskers saying, "Oops!"

El Gato let out a horrifying hiss. Everybody froze and stared, wondering what would happen next. El Gato's eyes shifted back and forth like he was thinking, *Is everybody staring at my tiny whiskers?* Then the crowd started murmuring, "Whiskers . . . walla, walla . . . whiskers."

El Gato forgot about being calmness. His claws popped out one by one and his tail puffed up to enormous proportions. He turned to Whiskers and said:

I threw myself between them. "El Gato, calmness is you!"

But El Gato only roared, "Angriness is me! ANGRI-NESS!" He pushed me aside and took another step toward Whiskers. Rosie came up beside me, kung fu paws at the ready, and said, "Let me at that bad cat."

"He's not a bad cat," I said. "Let me handle it." Then I picked up El Gato's whisker extensions, put my paw on his shoulder, and told him: "Here, pal! Put these on, and we can all go back to our happy place."

"YOU!" he said, his fur sticking out wildly in all directions. "You came here to ruin me and take my place! But it is I who will ruin you!!"

Then he pounced on me.

By the time I wriggled free, I
was a mess. I felt a bump rising on
the top of my head, and my bow tie
was severely askew. Worst of all, my
ears were turned inside out. And
you know how humiliating that is.

El Gato stood up, loomed over me, and said, "I am
El Gato. And you are a nobody!"

Those words were like a bright spotlight illumi-
nating the truth about El Gato. Maybe I was learning
something everybody else already knew, but the
important thing was I finally got it: El Gato was not
a nice cat.

Rosie tried to help me up but I shook her off. I
needed to do this on my own. I struggled to my feet,
straightened my ears, and finally spoke my truth: "I
may be a nobody, but at least I'm not a bully. Like
you."

Then I yanked off my polka-dot
bow tie, threw it at El Gato's feet,
marched out of the club, and
went out into the
night to discover
who I really was.

Tin Can Alley

I hit the streets of Hollywood running.

I ran like I was running from every dream that had turned to dust in my paws; like I could run back to that place where an innocent kitty named Mr. Puffball still believed in heroes. As I ran and ran and ran, the neighborhoods began to change. At first it was:

And then:

Before I knew it, I found myself in the city's dark underbelly. I stopped running and saw a group of those cats who come to Hollywood with big dreams, only to get chewed up and spit out into streets where streetlamps don't always work and often flicker.

Is this where I would end up? Would these poor souls be my new friends when El Gato made sure I never worked in this town again? I let out a melancholy sigh and moved on, wondering why I'd idolized El Gato for so long. I'd smiled when he tricked me into quicksand. I'd worn his heavy bling, even though it gave me a neckache. I'd even watched quietly as he tossed his fish tacos. Why?

Because it's hard to give up on your hero.

I was startled out of my thoughts by a growl emanating from the shadows. Oh, the horror, the horror! I'd wandered into *Dog Town*! The shadow took form and stepped in front of me. This guy was no miniature poodle, pug, or bichon frise. He almost made Bruiser look like a cat!

"Nice bump on your head, pal," he said.

"Are you talking to me?" I said. "Because I do not see anyone else around here.

So I assume you're talking to me."

He looked like he was trying to think up a good tough-guy comeback. But then we heard a loud burp. The rude dog turned to see who it was, and I ducked into a nearby alley. From behind a trash can, I watched the burper step into the streetlight.

It was El Gato!

"Well, well, well," said the dog. "If it isn't Puss in Cape."

"Good evening," said El Gato. "I am looking for my friend."

"Little fella with a bump on his head?"

"You've seen him?" said El Gato.

"Yeah," said the dog, "but he ran off. Anyway, he had nothing worth anything. But you got something I want."

"I don't have any doggie treats," said El Gato.

"To a dog like me, a new hat is a treat." He reached out and swiped the hat off El Gato's head. I waited for El Gato to go into his Kat Kong routine and knock that dog to Timbuktu, wherever that is. But he just took a step backward, toward the alley.

"I also like capes," said the dog.

"Please," said El Gato, backing farther into the

alley. "It's Corinthian leather."

"Excellent," said the dog, snatching El Gato's cape. "That leaves only the . . ."

"Not my mask," said El Gato, in a trembling voice. "I am El Gato, internationally famous actor. You may have seen me in such movies as—"

"I don't go to cat movies," said the dog. "And I want that mask." He yanked it off El Gato's face, making El Gato's eyes go very wide.

"Looks like I got it all," said the dog. "Except . . . what's that?"

El Gato pulled his paws toward his chest, and I spied a sliver of polka-dot bow tie. At this point, you may be wondering why I watched all this and did nothing. I had my reasons. I made a mental list of them and called it:

REASONS I DID NOTHING

1. The dog had big scary teeth and big scary paws. And bad breath.
2. El Gato could fight his own fights.
3. Why should I help El Gato after what he said to me?

But when I saw that polka-dot bow tie, I knew El Gato had followed me to return it and probably ask me to be his best friend forever. And that's when I said to myself, *Hey, don't just hide behind these smelly trash cans. Do something!* But what could I do? I was a nobody.

But then I remembered: I was not a nobody. I was Mr. Puffball, Stunt Cat to the Stars! And it was time for my biggest stunt of all.

By now, they were at the end of the alley. Along the alley ran a line of metal trash cans. Quiet as a cat, I jumped up and leapt from can to can. Along the way, I took one trash can lid in each paw. When I reached the end of the line, I catapulted myself into the air, and did this:

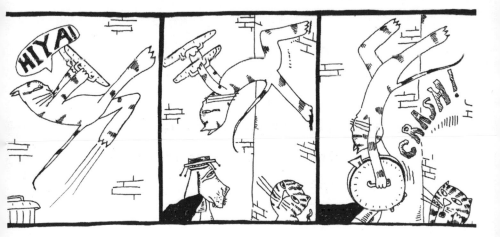

The bad doggie collapsed to the ground. I dropped the lids, wiped off my paws, and stood arms akimbo, like Supercat after he'd rid the world of evil dogs. I waited for El Gato to thank me, but when I glanced over, he was looking like he'd just realized he was in his birthday suit. Awkward!

El Gato did not thank me. He turned, picked up the trash can lids to cover himself, and ran away.

I knew I had to get out of there, so I yanked El Gato's clothes off the dog. I was barely out of the alley when an old car came rolling down the street. It was another dog, it had to be! *Should I throw the*

cape over myself and pretend to be an innocent lump or should I . . . My thoughts were interrupted by a familiar voice: "That was some stunt you pulled. Now get in here already."

Rosie! I climbed in, buckled up, and asked, "How'd you find me?"

"I drove around for hours looking for you. Then some street performer cats told me you'd gone this way."

"Thanks, Rosie. You're a real friend."

"So are you," she said. "Look, I hope you didn't believe what El Gato said. Everybody at the club thinks you're somebody special."

"And what do you think?"

She leaned over, gave me a kiss on the cheek, and said:

Now I knew it didn't matter anymore if El Gato was my hero or my costar or my frenemy. I had no reason to run. Rosie and my real friends made Hollywood my home, Gato or no Gato. When we pulled up in front of MGM Studios, I thanked Rosie. "You're awesome, too," I said. Then I got out of the car, walked up to the front door, and reached for the handle.

And that's when I heard a noise coming from behind the building that sounded like somebody gargling with hot sauce.

El Gato's Story

*I*t was El Gato, sitting in a cardboard box behind MGM Studios. When he saw me, he stopped yowling and said, "My mama used to sing me that song. I was singing it when Chet first found me, in this very box."

"Actually, I just put that out for recycling this afternoon."

He held up one paw. "Please, don't interrupt. I need to tell you my story." I sat on his cape to listen. "I was born in Tijuana, Mexico. Mama loved us, but we had nothing, so I went off in search of food, thrills, anything to fill my days and my belly. I fell in with some real tough alley cats.

"They dubbed me *Bigoticos*. It's Spanish for *tiny whiskers*. Always they bossed me: 'Find us squeaky toys, Bigoticos.' 'Hiss at that dog, Bigoticos.' 'Pass the

salt, Bigoticos.' Why did I obey? Maybe I thought I
didn't deserve any better, with my itty-bitty whiskers."

"Or maybe you just needed a hug," I said, but El
Gato gave me a look that said, *I do the talking now.
You do the keeping quiet*, and continued.

"One day they ordered me to catch some fish from
a river that ran through town. They knew I was scared
of water, what *gato* isn't? But they didn't care. 'Go.
Fish,' they said. So I went. I plunged both paws into
the river, knocking myself off balance in the process.

And then my nightmare came true: I fell in." El Gato shivered like he could still feel the cold water. "So *frio*, I can still feel it. What saved me? A branch floated by. I reached out and grabbed on and clung to it. And was swept away with the current."

"Why didn't you call for help?" I asked.

"I was too cold to mewl, too cold to wave, and I didn't have any flares. Anyway, nobody was there to hear me. Nobody was there to see me carried away from my family, my home, all the way across the border to El Norte."

"Where's that?" I asked.

"El Norte is this country, Mr. Puffball. The North. Now, please save your comments and questions until later. Anyway, days passed before the branch finally bumped up against the riverbank. I dragged myself out and made my way to San Diego. I went down an alley, saw an open door, and slipped inside. All I wanted was a place to dry off. I padded in and jumped onto a seat near a bucket of popcorn. I had never tasted popcorn before, and, to a hungry little kitten, it was like the food of the gods."

"Mmm," I said. "Popcorn."

"I was munching away when suddenly everything went dark. The big screen lit up, and there I was, watching my first movie ever. It was an old theater showing an old movie I will never forget: *Cleocatra Meets the Mummy.*"

"That was my—"

"Shh!" El Gato held up the *quiet, please* paw. "I fell in love with the movies that day and knew that I would do whatever it took to become a movie star. So I came to Hollywood and found Metro-Golden-Meower Studios . . ."

"Just like me!"

El Gato smiled. "Just like you, amigo. I spent the night back here—in this very box. Chet discovered me the next morning. I still remember what he said. 'Look at those adorable whiskers! Today is your lucky day, Gatito. I'm going to make you a star.'"

"Wow."

"Well may you say 'Wow.' I owe Chet a lot. He gave me my first big break in—"

"*A Tail of Two Kitties.*"

"With Meryl Stripe. But how did you know?"

"I know a lot about you. You're my hero. Or you were before . . ."

"Before I started acting like a jerk?"

"Yeah," I said. "But if Chet liked your tiny whiskers, why do you wear extensions?"

"I didn't wear them for my first movie. Or my second. But then I auditioned for Purramount. They were looking for a tabby with luxuriously long whiskers. Maybelline took pity on me. 'Come with me, Gatito,' she said. She worked on my whiskers for many minutes. And then she put a hat and mask on me. When she handed me that mirror, I knew I'd left Bigoticos and El Gatito behind forever. That was the moment I became *El Gato!*"

A bird chirped overhead. I hugged myself against the early-morning chill. And that's when El Gato said, "Get in here, friend. One cat alone will always be cold, but two in a box are forever warm. My mama told me that. But I almost forgot it."

"I've got your cape and stuff," I said, climbing in.

"And I've got your polka-dot bow tie," said El Gato.

"Thanks. But I still don't understand something. You had everything you wanted—fame, money, and long whiskers."

"So why was I such a hothead?" El Gato said. I nodded. "The day I became El Gato, I also became a cat with a secret. Over the years, my secret burned inside until I thought it would destroy me. I turned bitter and angry and not very nice."

"You almost attacked Whiskers. And he's the sweetest cat ever."

El Gato put his paws over his eyes. "I am not proud of my behavior. Indeed, Mr. Puffball, *I* am the nobody."

"Don't say that! Now I will tell a story. Long ago, in a little town called New Jersey, an adorable kitten saw a movie that changed his life forever: *Cow-Cats & Aliens.*"

"I was pretty good in—" El Gato started to say, but now it was my turn to hold up the *quiet please* paw.

"After that, the adorable kitten, who happens to be me, decided to watch every El Gato movie ever made. When that kitty saw you making fire in *Cats Away*, he was stranded on that island with you, feeling proud of what one cat can do with two dry sticks and a desire for salmon flambé. And when you were a fearless spy in *C Force*, he felt bionic, too, and believed he could run superfast and drive racecars. And when you single-handedly fought all those bad guys and saved the world in *Mad Manx*, so did he. Even though he was all by himself in his living room.

"C'mon, El Gato, you're a movie star! You're the stuff that dreams are made of."

"You really think so?"

"I know so. You were my hero, and, if I'm honest, you still are. Though if you could stop going all bossy-crazy-mean, that would be awesome."

"With a friend like you, Mr. Puffball, I feel I can do anything. Now, do you think they'd let us inside so we don't have to sleep in this ancient cardboard box?"

"Definitely."

"By the way," said El Gato as we headed in, "that was an amazing stunt you did to save me from the bad doggie. *Gracias*, amigo."

"A thank-you would also be nice," I said.

El Gato laughed. "I just thanked you in Spanish, Mr. Puffball. But I will do so in English as well: thank you, friend. We are friends now, aren't we?"

"The best of friends," I said. "By the way, that was my great-grandma Zelda in *Cleocatra Meets the Mummy*."

"Well, well," said El Gato. "So your great-grandma inspired me, and I inspired her great-grandson. Not bad."

We went inside. El Gato curled up in a basket near my bed. Then he pulled off the other half of his fake whiskers, winked at me, and said, "That's better." And even with the morning sun streaming through the window, we fell asleep at once.

My Debut . . . in 3D!

Later that day, after getting a lecture from Chet on the importance of respecting one's elders, peers, wait-staff, and "little kittens everywhere," El Gato said, "I don't want to be a bad cat anymore. I promise to try harder."

Kitty said, "That's all any of us can do."

Whiskers said, "Group hug!"

I said, "I love you guys!"

El Gato pointed to his whiskers and added, "And I'm done pretending to be something I'm not."

"So, you got small whiskers," said Chet. "I'm missing a patch of fur on my nose, but you don't see me making a big deal about it."

"I had my tail shortened so I wouldn't trip my dance partners," said Whiskers.

We all looked at Kitty. "Okay, Ms. Lola gave me extra stripes. So what?"

"You don't understand," I said, using my best leading-man kind of voice. "El Gato's luxuriously long whiskers are both his trademark and his burden. But now he's ready to show the world his true self. And I think we should help him!"

Everyone agreed, even before I told them my plan. It would involve some well-rehearsed drama-tization to take place at the opening-night party for *Nine Lives to Live*, only one week away. Think *Body Double* meets *Fencing with the Stars* meets *America's Craziest Stunt Videos*, and call it Opera-tion Tiny Whiskers.

When I laid out the details, El Gato loved my idea. "How can I ever repay you, friend?"

I told him he didn't owe me a thing, but a speaking part in *Nine Lives to Live* would be awe-some.

"I will make it so, Mr. Puff-ball."

Hooray! My upcoming debut would be as both actor and stunt

cat. Even if I didn't get an Oscar, or was only a nomi-
nee, I was finally living my dream.

I outlined my seven-day plan to prepare for Operation Tiny Whiskers and called it:

SEVEN-DAY PLAN TO PREPARE
FOR OPERATION TINY WHISKERS

1. Memorize lines.
2. Vocal coaching from Kitty.
3. Get Rosie involved, because she is a crucial
   element in the plan. Plus, she's cute.
4. Learn the art of fencing from Whiskers.
5. Convince Chet to make his directorial
   comeback.

Of course we made time for fun, too. Hula-dancing. Singing. Chet's story of how he'd lost that patch of fur on his nose (hint: *Keystone Kats* scene gone wrong!). And El Gato entertained us with his impression of that cat from *Shrek*:

That week flew by. It was time both for opening night of *Nine Lives to Live* and for Operation Tiny Whiskers. El Gato gave me a special gift for the occasion: a pinstriped suit with a matching zebra-stripe tie.

"Thanks a lot," I said. "Hollywood, here I come!"

I was ready for opening night, an important Hollywood event for any new movie, which can be broken down into the following list of elements:

1. Limousines and glamour galore
2. Celebrities and TV cameras
3. Movie critics crinkling candy wrappers in the back row

Our limo pulled up, and Rosie, Tabby Gaga, El Gato, and I walked the red carpet into the theater. Could it get any better? It could! The movie was in 3D.

The lights went down. The curtains went up. And that's when my heart started pounding like crazy. Because the opening shot was ME, larger than life. The narrator says,

"Sheriff Chad Manly searched the horizon for a mysterious cat he heard tell of." And then I say:

Rosie clapped and hooted. I did, too! Somebody shushed us, but I didn't care. I was too happy to be bothered by shushers, because I was finally watching a movie *I* was in. Plus, *Nine Lives to Live* had everything: stampeding snakes, dangerous cacti, evil kittens, unusual hats, heroic steeds, and death-defying stunts. And El Gato, who really is a great actor.

We laughed, we cried, we gasped, we ate popcorn. Somebody sneezed. We laughed again. Ate more popcorn. And cried one final time. It was the greatest night of my life.

Nine Lives to Live ended to uproarious applause, even before the credits started rolling by.

The critics jumped up, threw aside their jujubes, and instantly proclaimed it a smash hit! The movie portion of our evening was over.

But wait, there's more!

Because our biggest scene was yet to come.

Directed By
Cecelia B. DeMew

Produced By
Johnny Depp and Miso

Cast

EL GATO	ELGATO
Lightning	SiLVER
EL PERRO	REX
Billy the Kitten	TiGER
MEANINA	ROXiE
VERONiCA	TABBY GAGA
SALOON KEEPER	MOPSY
SNAKE #1	SUSiE
SNAKE #2	SASSY
SNAKE #3	WiLLOUGHBY
SHERIFF CHAD MANLY	MR. PUFFBALL

Story By
The Mysterious Ms. L.

Music By
Cat Calloway

EL GATO'S STUNT DOUBLE
Mr. Puffball

Lightning's Stunt Double
Thunder

Cactus Provided By
Cactus 'R' Us

Operation Tiny Whiskers

Anyone who was anyone was invited to the opening-night party at the Brown Tabby.

BRILLIANT MOVIE. EXCEPTIONAL CAST. WONDERFUL SCRIPT. NOW WHERE'S THE BRIE?

And they would all play a part in Operation Tiny Whiskers, whether they knew it or not. Someone famous once said, "All the world's a stage." Well, that night at the Brown Tabby, it sure was.

Inside, waiters bustled about with trays of shrimp cocktail, swordfish canapés, and sardine roll-ups. Balloons floated every-where, because it was Balloon Night. They danced in the light of the teardrop crystal chandelier, casting rain-bows in every direction. The giant fish tank had been specially stocked with elec-tric eels, Alaskan king crab, and miniature squid. Right beside the tank stood our "stage"—a long empty buffet table made of polished wood. The perfect setting for a bit of Reality Theater.

OMG, IS THAT BRAD KITT? HE OWES ME MONEY!

And our "audience" was ready.

IS MY DIAMOND TIARA GLITTERY ENOUGH?

MORE CAVIAR OVER HERE, WAITER, BEFORE THE MUSICIANS EAT IT ALL!

It was time to put Operation Tiny Whiskers into action. Here's how it went down—

Phase One: Chet moseys over to the fish tank. He raises his cane and raps on the glass three times, causing the electric eels to light up and the squid to squirt ink. Then he consults his paw (where he'd written his lines) and says loudly, "Hey, everybody! Where is El Gato?!" Kitty comes up beside him. She holds one paw to her forehead and scans the room. Then she sings, "Where, oh where, can he be?" We all hear a loud *beep*! Everybody turns as the ballroom doors burst open and in rolls the Catmobile with El Gato at the wheel. He steers toward the buffet table, waving to the crowd and running over some balloons along the way. The sound of popping balloons echoes through the cavernous room as Rosie rushes forward, points at El Gato, and says:

HE'S BACK!

Phase Two: El Gato jumps out of the Catmobile. He tosses back his cape, puts his paw on his hip, and surveys the crowd. "Yes. El Gato is back."

That was my cue. I float down from a catwalk above the stage holding three helium balloons. I'm dressed exactly like El Gato, down to my luxuriously long whisker extensions. I release the balloons one at a time until I land gracefully next to him and say, "Now El Gato is back."

At this point, all the cats in the Brown Tabby have gathered around us, spellbound by the unfolding drama. Some are still chewing their shrimp cocktail, but most are stock-still. Whiskers yells, "What's going on here?" and pushes through the excited crowd. He stops right in front of us, pointing one paw at El Gato and one at me. "One of you must **not** be El Gato! And I, for one, would like to know who!"

I pull out a sword and say, "I will be happy to show you who is who!"

El Gato draws his sword and says, "It is *I* who shall be happy, you imposter!"

Phase Three: The Epic Battle Scene. It begins with El Gato and I leaping onto the table and yelling, "En garde!" which is swordfighter lingo for "Let's do this thing!"

Then we put on a thrilling show! The "audience" loves our fancy legwork, elegant lunges, and powerful parries. They eat up our French phrases (*Touché! Allez! Attaque au fur!*) like they're French pastries. They gasp when I slice off El Gato's hat pom-poms. They groan when El Gato slashes at my Corinthian leather cape. Someone whistles when I write *I Am El Gato* in the air with my sword.

Phase Four (the Finale): El Gato's Big Stunt. The one we'd been working on all week. He takes a step backward and says, "Prepare to see the real El Gato!" Next, he turns and runs to the end of the table, pivots on the edge, and pauses a moment to smooth his whiskers. Then he races back and, when he's halfway to me, plunges his sword into the wood and polevaults into a perfect double flip. It's beautiful. As he passes directly over my head, I reach up, grasp his whiskers, and yank.

He lands like we cats always land: on his feet. Then we stand there, paws crossed over our chests— one El Gato with luxuriously long whiskers and one who is finally showing the world his itty-bitty ones. Chet points at El Gato with his cane and says, "Everybody knows El Gato has long, luxurious whiskers. So you, sir, are the imposter!"

"Oh really?" I say. Then, in one twirling motion, I whip off my hat, cape, mask, and whisker extensions until I'm wearing nothing but my birthday suit. I bow to El Gato, and he bows back. Then he launches into his speech.

"My name is El Gato, and I have tiny whiskers."

The audience gasps. Somebody laughs, but Rosie quickly shoves him into the Catmobile and slams the door. El Gato continues:

"I came to Hollywood because I love movies. Hollywood was very, very good to me, but I was very, very bad. Another cat came to Hollywood because he loves movies. He came with this"—El Gato held up tiny El Gato—"because he thought I was pretty cool. When we met, he discovered I was not cool. In fact, I was a hothead. But he stuck by me, this young cat.

And he turned out to be a great stunt cat, a talented actor, and a true friend. He has shown me the way back to my inner *gatito*. He has shown me it's not the whiskers that make the cat, it's what we do with them." El Gato put his arm around my shoulders. "Thank you, Mr. Puffball, for giving me the courage to be myself."

"Thank you, El Gato, for giving me back my hero," I said. "And for being my friend." And, just like at the movies, the crowd burst into wild applause. Someone even yelled, "We love you, El Gato!" Then somebody added, "And Mr. Puffball, too!"

"In that case," said El Gato, "fish tacos for everyone!"

Then the party really started! Tabby Gaga and Kitty sang a duet, and Whiskers showed us all how to do the twist. Just as I was twisting the night away, I glanced to my right and saw a familiar, wonderful face through a yellow balloon: Mom! If our reunion had been one of those old silent movies, this is how it would have looked:

I introduced my family to my friends. Then we all ate, laughed, and danced some more—the limbo, the mambo, hip-hop.

And of course it's not a party without the:

Could it get any better? Yes, it did! Because after the party, El Gato said, "You know, Mr. Puffball, my next movie is a buddy film. And you can't make a buddy film without a buddy. Right, buddy?"

There was only one thing I could say to that: "Wow."

THE END

. . . or is it?

SPECIAL FEATURES

THE HOLLYWOOD GAZETTE

★ ★ ★ ★ ★ ★ ★ ★ ★ ★ ★ ★ ★ ★ ★ ★

CELEBRITY OPINION PAGE

ROBERT REDFUR WITH NEW TINY WHISKERS

"I CAN'T BELIEVE I EVER WORE THEM LONG," SAYS THE STAR. "THESE TINY WHISKERS REALLY BRING OUT MY BABY BLUE EYES. PLUS THEY'RE EASIER TO CLEAN. I FEEL LIKE A NEW CAT! SO I'M CHANGING MY NAME TO RED. IT'S SHORTER, JUST LIKE MY WHISKERS."

CUPCAKE, A LOCAL KITTEN

VOICE OF A NEW GENERATION: "I HAVE LITTLE WHISKERS," SAYS THIS HOLLYWOOD NEWCOMER. "ALSO I LIKE STRAWBERRY ICE CREAM." THE YOUNG STAR-TO-BE SNEEZED VIOLENTLY BEFORE ADDING, "WHERE AM I?"

TODAY'S TOPIC: WHISKERS

A BARE-FACED TABBY GAGA!

"WHISKERS, WHO NEEDS THEM?" SAYS THE LATEST POP SENSATION. "I'VE TAKEN EL GATO'S FASHION STATEMENT ONE STEP FURTHER AND SHAVED MY WHISKERS CLEAN OFF. MY NEW LOOK IS DOTS. LOTS AND LOTS OF DOTS."

CHESTER P. GRUMPUS III WITHOUTA CLUE

OLDSTER REFUSES TO CHANGE: WE FOUND OLD DIRECTOR GRUMPUS ON THE SET OF HIS LATEST PROJECT, *SON OF A GREAT CATSBY*, TO ASK HIS OPINION ON THIS ISSUE. "I LOVE MY LONG KNICKERS, AND I'M NOT ABOUT TO GIVE THEM UP," HE SAID.

Glossary (According to the Author)

THE GIANT ANT WHO KICKED A SKYSCRAPER

Attack of the 50 Foot Woman (*Attack of the 50 Foot She-Cat) is a movie made in 1958, during the "Atomic Era," when Hollywood was crazy for things gone supersize due to atomic mishaps. There were movies about giant ants, giant squids, giant leeches, and giant mollusks (no kidding!).

Audition If you want to be in a movie and you're not George Clooney or Jennifer Lawrence, you have to audition. That means you read from a script, using your best dramatic gestures and expressions so the director will say, "Hey! We've found the next George Clooney/Jennifer Lawrence!"

Casablanca (*Catsablanca*) Made in 1942, *Casablanca* is considered by many to be the greatest movie of all time and much better than *Attack of the 50 Foot Woman*. It stars Humphrey Bogart, a true tough guy who said things like, "Here's looking at you, kid" and "Why don't you shut up? I'm getting hoarse listening to you" and "Please pass the salt. Now!"

HUMPHREY BOGART
(THE ONLY HUMAN EVER TO
LOOK TOUGH IN A BOW TIE)

Chanteuse is a fancy French word that means female singer. You could just say "lady singer," but wouldn't you rather say "chanteuse"?

CHANTEUSE

Conga Line is a marching dance from Cuba. Put your hands on the shoulders of the person in front of you (ask first!). Now, shuffle, shuffle, kick right! Shuffle, shuffle, kick left! You're doing the conga. (Don't you have homework to do?)

Crooner A crooner sings so romantically that everybody within earshot faints, cries, or at least stops kvetching. My all-time favorite crooner is Frank Sinatra, who is now crooning to the angels in the great beyond.

Director is to a movie as captain is to a ship. During filming, the director encourages the actors to act appropriately. He or she might say, "You've been struck by lightning, look surprised!" or "Dylan smashed your birthday cake, so cry already!" or "Somebody get that hedgehog off the set!"

Ear Trumpet is a real thing that I did not make up. They were widely used in the 1800s and beyond as rudimentary hearing aids.

EAR TRUMPET

A SMALL EXPLOSION

Explosives Expert is the person on set who makes things go *Kablammo!* or, for smaller explosions, *Blammo!* They score high on the Hollywood Jobs Coolness Graph. Obviously.

Finale is the big scene at the end of almost any performance. Picture every cast member dancing, juggling, tossing batons, flowers, confetti, etc. while singing, "A happy ending lets us know that life is not a bummer, and so we give our audience a fabulous last number!"

Gaffer is the head electrician in a movie or television crew. Personally I prefer "gaffer" to "head electrician." Sounds more mysterious!

The Great Gatsby (*The Great Catsby) is a classic American novel by F. Scott Fitzgerald. (Does the F. stand for Feline? Nobody knows!) It was made into a movie in 1974. Then somebody decided to do a remake of the movie in 2013. That's how great it is!

Grip is a movie tech person who secures and sets up tripods, dollies, and cranes (camera and lighting equipment). For example, "Hey, we need the grip to make  sure this camera travels across this unbelievably deep chasm without falling in!"

MOVIE CAMERA

Hobos are traveling workers, historically poor people who hopped freight trains, find-ing work where they could,

HOBO TOTE

especially during the Great Depression in the 1930s. There are still some hobos riding the rails, having conventions and even hobo parades.

Hula is a graceful Hawaiian dance form that tells a story. Some hula dancers wear leis, flowers in their hair, and shell bracelets. If you dance the hula, you are sure to feel the "Spirit of Aloha"!

The Jitterbug is a style of swing dance made popular in the 1930s and '40s. Ask your grandparents or other older friends if they did the jitterbug. They might just say yes. Or they might say, "Whither bug? Not in the pantry, I hope."

Jujubes are sticky, chewy candy in a rainbow of col-ors. I am not saying you should eat them (unless you want a mouthful of sweet chewy stuff).

Keystone Kops (*Keystone Kats) are comedic characters from the early days of cinema. They were police officers who did things like driving off piers and falling out of windows, off ladders, into water or mud and other hysterical antics, all while wearing ridiculous hats. Check them out on YouTube—I'm glad I did!

KEYSTONE KAP

Kvetch is a Yinglish (Yiddish/English) word which means complain. A classic example of kvetching is: "Two people are in a restaurant eating lunch. One says, 'The food here is terrible!' 'Yes,' agrees the other, 'and such small portions.'"

The Limbo is a dance from Trinidad where people ask themselves the age-old question "How low can you go?" as they bend themselves lower and lower beneath the limbo bar. Fun!

DANCING POTATOES

The Mashed Potato is a dance that does not involve potatoes in any way. Though my feeling is if potatoes want to dance, who am I to stop them?

Metro-Goldwyn-Mayer (*Metro-Golden-Meower) is a movie production studio founded in 1924. Over the years, they have made many, many, many, many, many, many, many movies. Their logo is a roaring lion, which is one of the reasons MGM is adored by cats the world over.

Monologue is a speech given by a single character. A classic example is by Marlon Brando in the movie *On the Waterfront*, where he plays an angry ex-boxer. His monologue ("I coulda been a contender, I coulda been somebody . . .") is poorly delivered by Mr. Puffball during his disastrous first audition.

My Fair Lady (*My Fair Kitty) is a movie musical from 1964. It was based on a Broadway musical that was based on a book that was based on ancient Greek mythology. It is considered by some to be the perfect musical, which proves that ancient Greek mythology is better when set to music.

Ollie is a skateboarding trick where you leap into the air with your board and yell, "Look, Ma! No hands!" only to discover that your mother has fainted.

SKATEBOARD

The Oscars is the greatest event in the world if you are nominated for one and especially if you win. They are yearly awards given by the Academy of Motion Picture Arts and Sciences for Best Actor, Best Director, or Best Glossary Writer. (Okay, not that last thing.) Winners walk away with a small golden statue. Glossary writers just walk away, probably to take a nap.

Producer is a movie's head honcho. The producer raises money to make the movie, hires important people, and says things like, "I thought this was supposed to be a comedy? Now!"

Paramount Pictures (*Purramount Studios) has produced many, many, many, etc. movies ever since 1912. "We Give You Something to Purr About" is not their motto. Yet.

Roswell is a city in New Mexico famous for being the site of a supposed 1947 UFO crash. Back then, people thought aliens were little green men in sil-

UFO

very spaceships. Of course, we now know that aliens are neon purple and travel the galaxy via cosmic dust (at least that's what I've heard!).

Silent Film In 1927, the first sound movie (or "talkie") was released. Before then, dialogue was written out on frames between action shots. For example:

Shot: A man holds flowers out to a woman.
His lips are moving.
Word frame: "Will you take these lilies?
They're making me sneeze."

Though movies before 1927 were silent, theaters were not. A musician, usually an organist, would play a musical score that suggested impending danger, kissing, or hedgehogs. Plus people ate Cracker Jacks, which are crunchy.

Solo A solo is when somebody sings alone and everybody else better keep quiet. Think of Judy Garland's beautiful rendition of "Somewhere Over the Rainbow." Imagine if Toto had howled along—everybody knows terriers can't sing!

Talent Scout is a Hollywood person on the lookout for talented people (or cats). So enunciate, dance, and sing loud; you might get discovered by a talent scout!

TNT stands for trinitrotoluene. I don't know how to pronounce it either. All I know is it makes things go *Kablammo!*

Triple Threat is exactly how Chet described it: a person (or cat) who can sing, dance, and act. Yoo-hoo! Mr. Talent Scout!

Uke is short for ukulele, a four-stringed instrument popular in Hawaiian music

UKE

and many other kinds of music. Ukes are cool! Haven't you ever heard the phrase "cool as a uke number"?

Watusi is a dance that was very popular in the 1960s. It's also fun to say—*watusi*. Try it!

* = Feline translation

Acknowledgments

Thanks to my parents, Rita and Joseph, for buying me art supplies even when the money was low. Thanks to my sisters for unbridled enthusiasm at all times. Thanks to my agent, Lori Nowicki, for seeing Mr. Puffball's potential when he was just an itty-bitty kitty. And to Claire Easton for your patience with newbie questions. Thank you, Jill Davis, for saying I'm SO CUTE (or were you talking about Mr. Puffball?) and for being the most awesome editor ever anywhere! And to Laurel Symonds for helping make it all happen. Much appreciation to Katherine Tegen for believing in *Mr. Puffball* from the start. Thank you, Amy Ryan, Katie Fitch, and Carla Weise, for making everything beautiful. Thank you, Lauren Flower, Rosanne Romanello, and Alana Whitman, for your marketing and publicity prowess. Thanks, Josh Weiss, for saying "MR. PUFFBALL" so enthusiastically and making it seem like it's your favorite book. Thank you, Ivy McFadden and Bethany Reis, for being copy-editors extraordinaire. Thanks, Megan Shepherd, for helping me figure out how to use my computer. Of course tons of thanks to the Secret Gardeners . . . you guys rock my world! Many loving thanks to Hank Bones for introducing me to Chester P. Grumpus III and everything else from brainstorming to art criticism. And thank you every day and always to my daughter, Madeline, for keeping it exceptionally real.

When **Constance Lombardo** was ten years old, her older sister did a lovely drawing. Not to be outdone, Constance did one too and hasn't stopped since. She drew posters for the high school drama club and cartoons for her high school newspaper. She did so many drawings, Syracuse University gave her a BFA in illustration, then politely asked her to leave. So she moved to New York City and drew people on the subway when they weren't looking. When they did look, she pretended to be knitting. Then Constance moved to San Francisco and painted on walls with a famous muralist. In 2003, she started reading picture books with amazing art (by William Steig, Beatrix Potter, and Arnold Lobel) to her kid. Not to be outdone, she began writing kids' books and hasn't stopped since. Constance enjoys drawing cats who are famous and infamous. Constance does not want another kitten. One is enough. This book is largely autobiographical, except that Constance is a human, never wears bow ties, doesn't eat fish, and is way too wimpy to do stunts. Constance hopes kids like old movies, because they teach us things like "In the old days, movies used to cost twenty-five cents!" and "In the old days, there weren't as many explosions!" The truth is, in the old days, your parents were quite young. Some of them weren't even born yet! She sure wasn't.